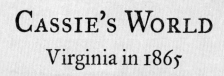

CASSIE'S WORLD
Virginia in 1865

Old wagon path

Cassie's farm

Secret thicket

Deserter's camp

Quaker cave

Apple orchard

Road to Danville

MYSTERIES THROUGH TIME

WATCHER IN THE PINEY WOODS

by

Elizabeth McDavid Jones

an imprint of

WINDMILL
BOOKS
New York

Published in 2009 by Windmill Books, LLC
303 Park Avenue South, Suite # 1280, New York, NY 10010-3657

This Edition copyright © 2009 Windmill Books
Text copyright © 2009, 2000 by Elizabeth McDavid Jones.

Cover and Map Illustrations: Jean-Paul Tibbles
Line Art: Greg Dearth

Photo Credit: Page 139, Library of Congress Prints and Photographs Division

Publisher Cataloging Information

Jones, Elizabeth McDavid, 1958-
    Watcher in the piney woods / by Elizabeth McDavid Jones.
        p. cm. – (Mysteries through time)
    Summary: In 1865, while helping her family keep their Virginia farm going through the end of the Civil War, twelve-year-old Cassie meets a Confederate deserter and a Yankee prisoner of war and tries to discover who has been stealing from the farm.
        ISBN 978-1-60754-304-6 – ISBN 978-1-60754-305-3 (pbk.)
ISBN 978-1-60754-306-0 (6-pack)
        1. Virginia—History—Civil War, 1861-1865—Juvenile fiction [1. Virginia—History—Civil War, 1861-1865—Fiction 2. United States—History—Civil War, 1861-1865—Fiction 3. Mystery and detective stories] I. Title II. Series
        [Fic]—dc22

Manufactured in the United States of America

To my parents, Bill and Joanne Huggins,
and my grandparents, Murl and Ruth Glenn Huggins

TABLE OF CONTENTS

CHAPTER I

POKE SALAD

It was because of poke salad that Cassie saw Myron first.

Everyone in the Willis family loved poke salad—poke greens simmered for hours with fatback and spring onions and served steaming hot—but nobody loved it more than Jacob, Cassie's seventeen-year-old brother. Jacob, of course, hadn't tasted Mama's salad in a very long time. Three years ago exactly, he had signed up with the Confederate army and marched away to whip the Yankees with General Johnston in Tennessee.

Today was only April eighth, early yet for pokeweed in Virginia, but Cassie had spotted some good tender poke shoots about a mile up the road from their farm. Mama had sent Cassie to fetch her some to make poke salad for supper. "You be careful though, Cassie," Mama had warned. "There's Yankees and no-good soldiers about—deserters and such. You know the Waldrops was robbed clean last week by a Yankee soldier out foraging. Keep Hector with you, hear? And don't go far." Hector was Cassie's dog, a hound given to her by Jacob before he left for the war.

That's how Cassie came to be up the road, bending over the fence around the tobacco field—now gone to dock weed and sheep sorrel—that Pa laid out right before he got drafted. "Won't be gone long," Pa had promised Mama. But he had already fought a year with General Lee, and there didn't seem to be much hope now of Pa coming home unless the war ended. Which it didn't show any signs of doing.

So here Cassie was, bent over double on Pa's fence, tugging at weeds growing by the side of the road, and feeling vexed about having to do it all herself.

Little Ben's help is no-account, Cassie was thinking. Though she dearly loved her four-year-old brother, he was an imp and always getting into trouble. Just this morning he had gotten himself a whipping for snitching one of Mama's ash cakes baked on the hearth. He took it from the windowsill where Mama had set it to cool and then fibbed about it to Mama.

Ben would have loved to tag along with Cassie, but his help was more trouble than it was worth most of the time. He would have picked the poisonous red poke shoots right along with the green, Cassie was sure.

Emma could have come, though, and helped—'course
she wouldn't, she was sixteen and prissy. And Philip, well,
there was no use asking him. Not the way he'd been boss-
ing everyone and putting on airs since Pa left him in
charge of the farm. Though only two years apart in age,
Cassie and Philip had never been close, and now it seemed
they did nothing but argue.

"Philip giving me orders all the time," Cassie fumed,
"like he was President Jefferson Davis instead of my
fourteen-year-old brother." She yanked hard at a stubborn
poke shoot and threw it into the basket that Mama had
given her.

Cassie looked wearily at the huge basket. It was
only half full. She straightened up and stretched an arm
behind her to rub the ache in her back, then pulled her
sunbonnet off her head and used it to wipe the sweat
that was trickling down her forehead. It was hot for an
April morning—seemed more like June. Hector, usually
frisky, was flopped in the shade of the pines at the edge
of the field. Cassie was of a mind to leave off picking
for a while and go down to the spring to cool her feet.
Maybe she could even find some lady's slippers or dogtooth violets in the woods to make up a bouquet for
the table.

While she was thinking, Cassie heard the clatter of a
wagon and spotted old Myron Sweeney and his nag Lucy
pulling out of the piney woods that circled the Willis land.

Myron had gone into Danville to pick up supplies for families in the vicinity whose menfolk were off at war, which meant practically everybody. So many things were scarce these days—from wheat flour to pins and needles— that the shelves of Sloan's store down at the crossroads were nearly empty. It was "make do with what you have or do without," Mama said.

But there just wasn't a way to do without some things that were scarce, like paper to write letters to Pa and Jacob on. Mama had asked Myron to see whether he could find some writing paper in town, and Cassie had given Myron the five cents she'd been saving from her Christmas stocking to get her some paper, too. She wanted to write Jacob a letter of her very own and tell him how much she missed him.

When Cassie caught sight of Myron, all the pains in her back disappeared. She whistled to Hector. "Come on, boy!" Then she left the poke greens and took off running to meet Myron's wagon. Hector sprang to life and raced after her.

"Whoa, young'un," Myron said. "Where you galloping off to in such a hurry?" Myron gave Cassie a hand up to the box seat beside him. "You done lost your bonnet again, girl. You're going to add another hundred freckles to that face." Hector trotted beside the wagon.

"Nary a soul would notice," Cassie said, "amongst all the freckles I already got." She pulled her sunbonnet back onto her head, though. No use having Emma light into her if she saw Cassie without it.

Myron had two or three small barrels piled in the back of his wagon, and what looked like a sack of flour. Cassie kept turning her head to look back there, hoping Myron would let on what he had brought for *her* family, but Myron didn't say a word. He just clucked to Lucy and turned up the corners of his mouth ever so slightly.

Cassie could hardly stand it. It wouldn't be polite to ask Myron flat out what he had brought, but maybe she could nudge him a little. "Looks like you got a heap o' stuff in your wagon, Mr. Sweeney."

Myron's eyes started dancing, and his long white mustache twitched. "I reckon I come away with more'n I expected to get," he said. "Let me see. What do I have back there?" He pulled on the end of his beard. "I got a sack of flour to be split between the MacKenzies, the Hefners, the Waldrops, and y'all. And a half pound of salt. Oh, and some wooden clogs for Maude Shope's young'uns. She wanted brogans for 'em, but ain't nobody in Danville got leather for shoes these days. What leather there is, the army gets."

Myron rambling on and on—Cassie couldn't bear it. "What else you got," she said, "for us?" Then she clapped her hand over her mouth. *How had such rudeness popped out from between her lips?* She had just broken a heap of Mama's rules of etiquette, all in one breath:

don't speak till you're spoke to, don't interrupt, don't be nosy, don't be sassy . . . Mama would be fit to kill if she'd heard Cassie.

But Myron only grinned. "Oh, you want to know what I got for *you*. Well, I wish you'd have said so. Why, I do believe there's a hoe blade back there for you. Yep, a hoe blade. So you can get to work on your Mama's kitchen garden."

Cassie knew times were tough, but she had been so hoping . . . She swallowed hard and tried to hide her disappointment. "Reckon we do need a hoe blade. Philip tried to whittle one out of a hickory branch. Didn't work too well." Cassie dropped her chin. She didn't want Myron to see the tears she felt welling in her eyes.

Myron's eyes quit dancing, and he put his hand on Cassie's knee. "Couldn't get no writing paper, Cassie. I hate it. I know you was counting on it." Then his mustache twitched again, and he added, as if he'd only just remembered it, "However, I come across something in town that might go a ways towards making up for that lack of writing paper."

Curiosity replaced Cassie's disappointment. "You did? What is it?"

Myron reached back and pulled something out of the hip pocket of his britches—an envelope. He held it up, and with a smile that could have spread across the whole state of Virginia, he said, "It's from North Carolina.

You know anybody from down in them parts?"

Cassie's heart leaped. "Jacob!" Last they had heard from Jacob, he was still with General Johnston, being chased by that Yankee general Sherman across the Carolinas. That was over three months ago, and there had been no word since. They'd all been worried sick about him. Now at last to know that Jacob was safe . . . Cassie's insides felt near to bursting.

"Can I see it?" she asked, then quickly added, "Please."

"Why sure," Myron said. "I was thinking you should be the one to give it to your mama anyway, seeing as how you and Jacob was always so close."

Cassie stretched out her hand eagerly. The envelope looked like it had been made from wallpaper. One more way of making do, Cassie figured. On the outside was scrawled Mama's name—Annie Willis—and then just *Danville, Virginia.* Cassie wondered why Jacob hadn't sent the letter straight to Sloan's store, like he usually did. That way Mama would probably have had it a week or more ago.

But, Cassie thought, *the main thing is we got the letter now.* She held it tightly while Myron's wagon bounced down the narrow, rutted road toward the Willis farm. Finally, they wound around through the pecan grove, and Cassie spotted the little weatherboard house with the green roof—home.

Jacob had surprised Mama for her birthday one year by painting the shingled roof bright green. He did it while Pa and Mama were in town. Pa was mad at Jacob for wasting time and money on such foolishness, but Mama liked it. She said the roof reminded her of spring all year round. The green roof made Cassie think of Jacob's generous ways, and she pressed the letter even closer to her chest.

Nobody was in sight when the wagon finally rolled up to the front gate. "Mama!" Cassie yelled, half to make herself heard over the racket of the wagon and half because she couldn't keep quiet another second. "Where you at? Emma! Philip! Ben! Come quick! Come and see what Myron brung us!"

Cassie jumped off the wagon before Myron even reined Lucy in. "It's a letter! From Jacob!" Hector, caught up in Cassie's excitement, barked and frisked at her feet.

Ben let out a whoop from somewhere back of the kitchen. The kitchen was a separate building set away from the main house.

Then Cassie saw the kitchen door fly open, and Emma burst out and hurried across the yard. Mama came behind Emma, walking slow and dignified, like she always did. She greeted Myron with an outstretched hand.

"Mornin', Myron. Did you have a nice trip?" Mama's voice was unruffled, as if Cassie clutched a bucket of taters and not a letter from Jacob. Cassie felt so impatient she could hardly stand it. How could Mama be concerned with being polite at a time like this?

"Mama," Cassie said, holding the envelope up. "Here it is. The letter from Jacob."

Mama put her hand on Cassie's shoulder. "Patience, sugarfoot. Mr. Sweeney come a long way with news of my oldest boy. The least we can do is greet him proper."

"That's all right, Miz Willis," said Myron. "You go right ahead and read that letter. We'll save our howdy-dos for later, after me and Philip get the wagon unloaded."

Philip had come from the barn and was standing behind Mama. His shirt and britches were caked with red mud. He looked dog-tired. Cassie had forgotten that Philip had spent the morning digging stumps out of the new cornfield. All by himself. Cassie's conscience pricked her. Being left in charge of the farm wasn't such an easy thing, she reckoned.

"Here, Mama." Cassie pushed the envelope toward Mama again, and this time Mama took it. It was nice to see Mama smiling, not just bows at the corners of her mouth, but a big, wide smile that showed her teeth and made her face look like the sunrise over Oak Ridge. Like she used to smile before Pa and Jacob left. Like before the war.

But when Mama looked close at the envelope, her eyebrows knit together, and she said, "Peculiar. This don't look like Jacob's handwriting."

Myron frowned. "It come from North Carolina. So I just reckoned it was from Jacob. Who else do y'all know from there?"

"Well, surely it's from Jacob," Mama said, but she gave Myron a little smile that Cassie didn't think she felt. Then Mama tore open the envelope. Her hands were trembling.

Cassie stood and watched Mama's eyes go back and forth over the letter. Mama's lips moved silently, forming the words. Then Mama's face went white, and her lips stopped moving. Cassie felt a stab of fear.

Mama closed her eyes and pressed the pale pages against her chest. Cassie wanted fiercely to ask Mama what had put that look on her face, but she couldn't find her voice to do it.

Emma had no trouble finding hers. "What is it, Mama? What's wrong? Is the letter from Jacob?"

Emma's words hung frozen in the air. No one moved. Cassie couldn't even breathe. She looked at Mama and waited.

Finally Mama opened her eyes. "Philip, help Myron tote them things from his wagon," she said, but the life had gone out of her voice. She sounded like she did after the Home Guard came and hauled Pa off to fight with General Lee. It hurt Cassie to hear Mama sound that way again.

Mama turned then and walked away, her shoulders

sagging. She walked right on back to the kitchen, forgetting to invite Myron to dinner, forgetting to thank him, forgetting to tell him good-bye and see him off. Cassie couldn't believe it. Not once had she ever seen Mama forget her manners.

Cassie stood where she was, watching Mama go. They all stood there—even Ben—staring after Mama. Emma's chest was heaving up and down, and Myron looked sick, like he'd gotten punched in the stomach. A long minute passed, and then suddenly Emma jumped forward and started after Mama. Philip moved silently to the wagon and reached for a barrel.

"Mama!" Cassie called, and ran after her. Emma glared, as if Cassie had no right to speak to her own mother.

Mama turned and looked at Cassie with empty eyes. "What is it, Cassie?"

Everything Cassie wanted to say flew from her brain. "I . . . I forgot the poke greens," she stammered. "Want me to run back and fetch 'em for you, Mama?"

"Don't want no poke greens," Mama answered in that dead voice.

Cassie felt desperate. All of a sudden, those poke greens seemed greatly important. "But you was going to make poke salad, remember?"

Mama, oh, Mama, Cassie thought. *If you would just go on and fix your poke salad tonight. Make everything better again, Mama. Please.*

"Poke salad?" Mama said. "I don't never want poke salad again, you hear?"

Then Mama pulled up the latch on the kitchen door, went in, and shut the door behind her, leaving Cassie and Emma standing, bewildered, on the steps.

CHAPTER 2
THE LETTER

All through dinner, Mama was silent. Silently she laid four places at the long oak table in the kitchen; silently she set down bowls of food—steaming sweet potatoes, cornbread, pickled tomatoes.

Then, without a word, she hauled herself to the rocking chair in the corner and rocked back and forth, staring into empty air.

Cassie sat at the table, with her brothers and Emma, going through the motions of eating, but she had no appetite. All she could think about was Mama and the way she was acting and the letter that had started it all.

After dinner, Mama sent them all to the house to wait for her. She wouldn't say why, but Cassie figured she was going to tell them what was in the letter. "I'll be in directly," Mama said, though she kept right on rocking.

To Cassie, it was an eternity that the four of them—
five, counting Hector sprawled on the hearth—waited
for Mama in the sitting room. The hands of the old
planter's clock on the wall seemed to barely budge. Ben
sat with Hector by the hearth, playing in the ashes, and
when he asked for the fifth time, "When's Mama coming?
She said she was coming," Philip blew up and told him
he was peskier than a big black horsefly. Ben started to
wail, and at that moment the door opened and Mama
came in.

Mama paid no heed to Ben, which wasn't like her at
all. "I reckon we got us a letter to read," was all she said.
She marched over to the slat-back rocker and sat herself
down. Ben took one look at Mama and hushed right up.

As Cassie watched Mama, she suddenly had a vision
of the big basswood tree on their land that got struck
by lightning a few years back. The tree stood tall and
straight on a ridge beyond the cornfield, dwarfing all
the other trees around. But it never did bear leaves
again after getting hit, and although it looked strong
on the outside, Cassie figured that tree felt right pitiful,
stripped bare and all alone like that. Mama was that
tree, trying to look strong but not feeling that way,
Cassie thought.

In a voice that sounded too light and breezy, Mama
started reading. "Dear Mrs. Willis," she read. She stopped
and clutched at her throat, then squeezed her eyes shut.

The planter's clock ticked, ticked, ticked. Fear built steadily in Cassie's chest.

Finally Mama's eyes opened, and she began once more. This time she read straight through:

Goldsboro, North Carolina
March 15th, 1865

Dear Mrs. Willis,

Please forgive the crude appearance of this correspondence. I wanted to jot down these lines and send them out to you swiftly, and, as no proper paper was available, I used this bit of wallpaper that my hostess so kindly provided for my sad purpose.

For the last year I have had the privilege of commanding the regiment in which your son Jacob has served. I could never speak highly enough of Jacob's integrity and his courageous conduct on the battlefield. No, I could never speak highly enough, for it was Jacob who saved my life in a skirmish with the enemy near here on March 10th. He pulled me out of a storm of artillery fire and took a ball in the chest for his efforts. I was badly wounded myself and nearly senseless; my last impression is of your son bending over me and covering me with the gray greatcoat you sent him last winter.

When I regained consciousness, I found myself in a local home, which was being used for a hospital.

It was here that I learned the unfortunate fate of your son. Our troops had been forced to retreat suddenly and hurriedly, and our dead and the mortally wounded had to be left behind. Jacob, I'm told, was one of those who died.

After that, Cassie's brain shut down. She was in a pond, she felt, floating facedown and looking through murky water to the bottom. She heard and saw what was going on, but only through a haze. She heard Mama going on with her reading, heard the sound and rhythm of Mama's voice, but Cassie's mind recorded nothing. She felt her eyelids blink. She was aware of her own breathing: in, out, in, out. She heard someone shrieking and let her eyes move across the room. It was Emma; Emma was sobbing into her hands. Cassie blinked again. Then she realized that the rhythm of Mama's voice had stopped. There was no sound in the room but Emma's sobbing.

Then Cassie heard Ben speak. "What's wrong with Emma?" he asked. Cassie's eyes followed the sound of his voice to the hearth. She noticed that his hands were black with soot.

At first nobody answered. Mama had her elbows propped on the arms of the rocker. Her hands covered her forehead and eyes.

Ben hopped up and ambled over to Emma, leaving

black, sooty footprints on the pinewood floor. "Why you crying, Emma?" He put a sooty hand on Emma's knee and lowered his head to look into her face.

Emma jerked away and put her head down on the writing desk. Ben looked hurt. He swiped at a shock of yellow hair hanging in his eyes, which left a black streak on his face. "What's wrong, Mama? What's wrong with Emma?"

Mama sighed. "She's sad, sugar."

"Why, Mama?"

"'Cause your brother Jacob ain't coming home from the war."

"Don't he like us no more?"

"No, sugar. It ain't that."

"Then what?"

Mama seemed barely able to force out the words. "He's gone. Gone up to heaven."

"How'd he get there?"

Mama squeezed her eyes shut again. Then, before she could answer, Philip was up, had Ben by the hand, and was bellowing at him. "I'll tell you how he got there! A stinking, yellow-bellied Yankee shot Jacob down like a dog."

Ben's eyes got as big as a full moon. Philip went on. "Them damn Yankees killed him, boy. They killed your brother dead."

Ben started to whimper.

"Philip, that's enough," Mama said.

Philip kept on like he didn't even hear Mama. "I'll get 'em back someday. You watch me. I'll kill me a Yank. I will. "

By then, Mama was standing. Her shawl had fallen off and lay in a heap on the floor. Her eyes flashed fire at Philip. "You hush your mouth right now, boy. What's got into you, spewing out that hateful talk, scaring your little brother? We don't act like that in this family. No matter what happens."

Philip slid his jawbone back and forth. He was struggling; he wanted to say something back to her, but he didn't dare. So he looked around at everybody and said, "Y'all always finding fault with me. 'Spect me to work like a man, but you treat me like a boy. Pa setting me in his place—that's a joke. Ain't nobody treats me like they would him."

All of a sudden, Cassie's mind cleared. Rage at Philip boiled up out of her throat. "Why don't you quit thinking about yourself?" she said. "This ain't about you! It's about Jacob. So what if some lying letter says he's dead? I don't believe it! I don't!"

"Cassie—" said Mama.

"No, Mama. It ain't true. I'd know if he was dead. I'd feel it."

Mama opened her mouth to speak. Cassie didn't give her the chance. "He ain't dead!" Cassie said. Hector's head jerked toward Cassie. He jumped up and trotted to her side. Cassie let her hand fall to Hector's neck. She heard Jacob's voice ringing in her head: "A puppy for you, Cass, to take my place on your treks through the woods. So you won't be lonesome while I'm gone . . ." The memory pressed down on her, heavy as an anvil on her chest. Her breaths came quick and short.

Philip, his face hard, said, "You're the one that's lying, Cassie, and you know it."

Mama started to walk toward Cassie. "Listen to me, honey."

Cassie was sweating—it was so hot in that room— and she couldn't breathe. She couldn't bear to hear what they were saying. She clapped her hands over her ears and backed toward the door. "No. Please," she said. "Don't talk to me!" Then she turned and bolted outside. Hector scrambled out the door with her before it slammed.

"Cassie!" It was Mama, calling after her, but Cassie didn't look back. Around the side of the house she raced, Hector loping beside her, through the gate, and across the road, running, running, out to the pecan grove, and on.

Where she was headed, Cassie didn't know. Any place would have done, any place where she could get away from the mallet hammering the terrible words into her brain: *Jacob is dead . . . Jacob is dead.*

On Cassie ran, into the piney woods, up an ancient, rutted wagon path, to the old apple orchard, where the tree trunks were blanketed with moss and the ground was covered with periwinkle. By now a purpose had formed in her mind, a destination. She was going to the thicket—of course—the secret hideaway in the woods that she and Jacob had shared.

Winded, Cassie slowed to a jog, through a thicket of cedar trees and broomstraw, up a stony pine ridge to the deep woods. Everything here, where she and Jacob had played and explored for countless hours, reminded Cassie of him. A clump of pine saplings made her think of the way he used to bend saplings over for her to ride on like a pony. Partridges whistling brought to her mind the time the two of them found a partridge nest and brought the eggs home to Mama so she could make custard.

The memories sliced into Cassie with sharp, searing pain, and she broke into a run again, through the briers and all. She stopped at the spring—she had to get a drink; her throat ached something awful and was so tight she could hardly breathe. She cupped her hands, slurped up the icy springwater, and gulped it down so fast, it made her throat hurt worse. Then she called to Hector and headed on up the hill toward the secret thicket.

Jacob had hollowed out the thicket when he was twelve years old, the same age as Cassie now. He'd cut out a circular opening inside a stand of witch hazel shrubs and rose acacia bushes and hacked two secret entrances through the wisteria vines that tangled around the shrubs.

Later on Jacob showed Cassie the thicket, and after a while it became "their" secret place. When Jacob went away to war, Cassie had promised herself she'd look after the thicket until he came back—keep it from growing over, and keep it secret. She had kept her promise for three long years.

Hector ran ahead of Cassie. By the time she spotted the circle of shrubs that enclosed the thicket, Hector had disappeared through one of the secret entrances. The dogwoods and redbuds had bloomed since the last time she was here, and they blazed, gorgeous, in pink and red across the hill. The wild plums and the cherry laurels were also in bloom, and the air was filled with the smell of honeysuckle. Clumps of red and yellow columbine and tiny white spring beauties flourished everywhere.

"It's too beautiful," Cassie whispered. "It shouldn't be like this, not with Jacob gone."

Hector barked from inside the thicket. Cassie tugged at the wisteria vines until they gave way, and crawled through an opening to the clearing inside the thicket. Hector was lying against an old log on the thicket's floor, sunning himself. She threw herself down beside him and rested her head on the log.

Cassie's feelings were all tangled up inside her, and it hurt too much to try to sort them out. She didn't *want* to try; she would rather close them away and never have to think about them.

If only she could hide here in the thicket forever, shut off from everyone else, shut off from this nightmare they called a war . . . As long as she was here, Jacob would be alive. He'd be whistling tunes and telling jokes somewhere, making the other soldiers laugh, and talking about how he couldn't wait to get home to his little sister Cassie.

Oh, if only she could.

For a long time Cassie lay there, dry-eyed, against the log. She couldn't cry. She watched a hawk, far above, curling through the sky. She listened to the woods, still but not still—there, the faintest wind breathing through the trees; there, the distant yelp of a wild turkey.

She remembered all the hours she had spent with Jacob here in the thicket, playing or talking, or just listening, like she was doing now. She thought of the last afternoon before Jacob left for the army, when she had looked for him and found him here and they had stayed for hours and talked.

It was summer then, in '62; Jacob was barely fourteen. He hadn't said a word then of soldiering. All he talked about was home, things they'd done, good times they'd had. She was too young then—only nine—to think much about it. But now, when she considered it, it seemed more and more to her that Jacob hadn't really wanted to go to war at all.

"Why did he go?" she whispered, her heart aching. "If he didn't want to, why did he go?"

Cassie closed her eyes. What she wanted most was to see Jacob's face again, if only in her mind. She tried to remember, to picture him on the chilly gray morning when he had left. She pressed her eyelids together and concentrated hard. But the only picture that would come to her mind was another face—her own—reflected in the brass buttons of Jacob's uniform jacket.

The jacket was homespun, dyed yellowish-brown with butternuts, and sewed by Mama and Emma in their neat, tiny stitches. There were six buttons on it. And six blue-eyed, snub-nosed faces stared back at Cassie when she looked at them.

And that was all Cassie could remember. She could see as clear as a summer sky those little round Cassie faces gleaming from Jacob's buttons. But for the life of her, she could not conjure up a picture of his face.

Then Cassie cried.

Waves of sobs boiled up from the anguish within her, and kept coming, and coming, until Cassie's insides felt empty, and she was very, very tired. It occurred to her then that she should be getting home. Who knows how long she had been here? Yet she couldn't find the strength to move.

Sometime while Cassie was crying, Hector had stirred from his place in the sun, come to her, and laid his head on her leg. Now Cassie stroked the spot under Hector's chin where he liked to be scratched, and she happened to glance at the flattened leaves where he had been lying. She saw something glinting in the sun there, something round and shiny—a button, it looked like, a brass button.

"How did that get here?" she said aloud. She reached out and picked up the button, cupped it in her hand. It was a plain, ordinary brass button, scratched, with most of the finish worn off. It looked like it might have come off someone's good suit of clothes or off a uniform, a soldier's uniform.

"Ain't that curious, Hector? A button here? When nobody knows about this place 'cept you and me?"

But buttons, Cassie knew, didn't turn up in thickets all by their lonesome. *Somebody* had been here.

Mama's warning leaped to Cassie's mind: *Yankees and no-good soldiers about . . . don't go far.*

Cassie bit her lip and looked at the button again. She turned it over and over. It could belong to anyone. But it *did* look like a soldier's button, didn't it? And soldiers were passing through all the time—cavalry scouts, messengers, troops on the move. But those soldiers were doing just that—passing through. No decent, honorable soldier would leave his regiment and come out to the deep woods all alone. And no decent, honorable soldier would go crawling around in a thicket either.

Cassie felt a twinge of fear. She had heard plenty of stories about rogue soldiers—escaped prisoners, deserters, and slackers, both Yankees and Confederates, who hid in the woods and roamed the countryside, stealing, plundering, and worse . . .

A shiver went down Cassie's spine. Whoever had been here in the thicket was someone who was up to no good. And there was no way to tell when that someone might come back.

CHAPTER 3

ALONE IN THE SWAMP

Cassie's heart thumped against her ribs. She clenched the button tightly in her fist. How long had the button been here? A week? A day? An hour? Maybe the soldier who had dropped the button—Cassie had already begun to think of him as a soldier—was somewhere nearby even now, *watching her.*

Something rustled in the shrubs behind her. Seized by panic, Cassie dived for the passageway and scrambled outside, just in time to see a startled chipmunk dart away from the thicket. Hector sprang after the creature, barking, but the chipmunk disappeared into a hole.

"Mercy," Cassie said. She sank to the ground and tried to still her racing pulse. She'd been scared for nothing—this time. But she wasn't about to wait around for someone who was a real threat to show up.

"Let's get on home," she said to Hector. She dropped

the button into her pocket and added, "Real quick." She had already decided to take the fastest route back to the farm, which meant a shortcut through the huckleberry swamp. The swamp crawled with water moccasins and rattlers, but poisonous snakes seemed less frightening than the faceless image of the rogue soldier that loomed in her mind. Besides, Hector would give her fair warning before she stepped on a snake. Cassie picked out a big stick to carry, though, just in case.

At the bottom of the hill, she turned east instead of south, and it was less than a mile to the swamp. The swamp, dotted with creamy white huckleberry blooms, looked almost inviting. Hector must have thought so; he plunged right in. Cassie started after him, following a deer trail through the tangle of huckleberry shrubs, past tall canes of swamp rose and snakeroot rising on long purple spikes. A ways into the swamp, her stomach began hurting—whether from hunger or fear, she didn't know—and the farther she hurried through the muck and briers, the harder it was to ignore the pain.

Cassie spotted a copse of sassafras trees just off the trail, on a little hummock at the edge of the swamp. Sassafras was the best thing for a stomachache, Mama said, so Cassie decided to get some sassafras bark to chew on. "This way, boy," she said to Hector, and started up the hummock.

When she got to the top, she saw that on most of

the trees, the bark was infested with some sort of bug. As she pushed farther into the copse searching for some unblighted bark, she spied what looked like a shelter rigged up next to a little pawpaw tree. Taking a few steps closer, she could see it *was* a shelter: a blanket, raised a few feet off the ground by sticks to form a little tent. The other side was tied to some low branches of the pawpaw tree. Pine boughs had been piled on top of the blanket to hide it. Outside the shelter was a circle of blackened ground and charred wood, the remains of a campfire. A wooden canteen hung from the limb of a tree nearby.

Then Cassie saw something that made her mouth go dry. Slung on the ground a few feet from the campfire were a military haversack and a soldier's forage cap.

This was a soldier's campsite.

Was it the same soldier who had trespassed in her secret thicket?

Fear twisted in Cassie's belly. She had the urge to run, but she made herself stay. Apparently there was no one around. Hector didn't seem the least bit alarmed. He had already rushed forward to sniff at the campfire.

Cautiously Cassie followed Hector. She bent to touch the charred wood; it was cold. There'd been no fire here for a while, anyway. Where was the soldier who had made the shelter and left his belongings? And *who* was he? The fellow was obviously hiding; why else would he camp smack-dab in the middle of a swamp? He was a no-good, that was for sure, probably a deserter. Maybe he was the Yankee who robbed the Waldrops, claiming to be foraging for supplies for his troops. "Foraging," Cassie knew, was the Yankees' way of stealing from everyday folks without calling it such.

Cassie felt a little braver now, and curious, very curious. She moved forward to get a closer look, crouched, and picked up the haversack. Strange—it was empty. Hector pushed past her and sniffed at the haversack. Then he caught sight of a rabbit in the brush at the edge of the clearing and took off after it. In an instant both Hector and the rabbit had disappeared down the side of the hummock.

Cassie was puzzling so over the haversack, she scarcely noticed Hector was gone. Usually soldiers carried personal items in their haversacks, like mess kits, sewing kits, razors, and handkerchiefs. It was odd, she thought, that this haversack was empty. What did it mean? Had the soldier been forced to abandon his campsite? He must have gone in a hurry, to leave his hat and canteen—valuable articles for a soldier.

Cassie eyed the hat. It was bedraggled and filthy, encrusted with mud, and a color that she couldn't name. Had it once been Yankee blue or Rebel gray? There was no way to tell, not now. Likely it had been blue, she thought, for it would be like a Yankee to slink away and hole up like this in the woods.

Then the canteen, twisting slowly in the breeze, caught Cassie's eye. For the first time she noticed there were letters painted on its side. She watched as the canteen twisted away, then back again. Now she could see the letters clearly: *CSA* — Confederate States of America.

Cassie's stomach lurched. This no-good deserter was a Confederate — one of their own. He was *supposed* to be fighting for the South. Yet brave soldiers like Jacob were being killed, while this fellow ran away.

Cassie felt sick with the knowledge, but angry, too. "It'd serve the coward right to be hauled off to Danville and turned over to army headquarters," she said aloud. "To be shot, like he deserves."

Then Cassie jumped half out of her skin as she felt her arms pinned behind her. A voice, thick and gravelly, said, "Now, missy, you wouldn't want to see a thing like that happen, would you?"

Paralyzing fear shot through Cassie's body. Her brain froze.

"What you doing here?" The man's voice was angry.

He pulled Cassie's arms tighter behind her, nearly wrenching her shoulders from the sockets. White-hot pain yanked Cassie's brain back to life.

"Quit! That hurts!" Cassie jerked her head around fast to see who had hold of her, but he was faster. He tightened his grip on her.

"Turn me loose!" Cassie said. She kicked at his shins. He buckled. She tore one arm free and wriggled like a night crawler to pull away the other arm. His grip on her arm turned to iron, and his fingernails pressed into her wrist. His other hand, Cassie saw, was on the hilt of a knife strapped to his belt.

"I wouldn't do that again, missy," he said. "Wouldn't try to run neither, if I was you. I ain't killed a young'un yet, but my pappy claimed there's a first time for everything. Don't do anything stupid to make this my first time." The man released Cassie with a shove. "Now tell me what you doing here," he said again.

Fear made Cassie's knees weak, but she turned and forced herself to look at the man, to look him over good. He wasn't tall, but he was built stocky, with broad shoulders and a wide chest. He looked like he had once been muscular, but now he was gaunt, with sallow skin. He was dressed in a dark homespun butternut, like half the Southern army. His britches were torn off at the knee, and sores oozed where his brogans cut into his ankles. The front of his uniform was ripped, and—Cassie's breath caught in her throat—some of the buttons were missing off his jacket.

"You best speak when you're spoke to," the man was saying. "You best answer me."

Cassie kept her silence. She didn't owe him an answer; she didn't owe him anything.

"Cat got your tongue, has it?" The man took a step closer. He stank of sweat and swamp water. "Tell me, girl. What you doing out here in this swamp?" He spit the words in Cassie's face. His fists were balled. "Answer me!"

Cassie's pulse was pounding in her throat. "It's a short-cut home," she said. She prayed her voice didn't betray her fear.

"Home." The man's lips parted in a menacing grin. His yellow teeth gleamed. "Now where might that be?"

"None of your durn business!" she cried.

He backhanded Cassie across the face. "Mind your manners when talking to your elders, girl. Ever' one of my eight young'uns got better manners than you."

Tears leaked from Cassie's eyes, but she blinked them back. She couldn't believe this stinking polecat was some-body's pa.

The man spit, then glowered at Cassie. "Now I got to figure what to do with you," he said, "being as how you've a mind to see me shot for desertion." He seated himself on a tree stump and propped one bony leg on the other. "Being as how you've discovered my little homestead here."

"What *you* better do," Cassie said, "is get yourself on out of these woods 'fore you get caught. Don't you know there's soldiers swarming all over this county? I seen a passel of soldiers up at Sloan's store yesterday."

"Them soldiers ain't going to come near this snake-infested pit," said the man. "It's just me and the rattlers here, and I like it that way. Ain't nobody bothered me yet, nobody but a busybody young'un." He pulled his knife from its sheath and plunged it into the stump. "What kind of ma you got," he snarled, "that she didn't learn you not to poke your nose in other folks' business? Good-for-nothing, ain't she?"

At that insult to Mama, Cassie's hackles flew up, and words were out of her mouth before she could stop them. "One thing she learned me was the difference between a good soldier and a yellow-bellied coward!"

Cassie's chest went tight as she realized what she had said. Alarmed, Cassie swept her gaze to the knife, expecting to see the deserter's fingers closed around it. But he surprised her. He took his hand off the knife. The corners of his mouth turned up. Cassie might have called it a smile, if it hadn't chilled her to the bone.

"Got me pegged a coward, do you?" he said. "Well, now, I wonder what *you'd* do, little lady, when the shells started flying and the bullets started zinging past your sweet little ears. And men was screaming in pain and dying all around you. What would you do?" His fingers went back to the knife and tapped against it.

Cassie's heart pounded. She couldn't have spoken if she wanted to.

After what seemed forever, the deserter dropped his hand. "Reckon," he said, "you might just turn and run, like

I done. You might. If you was smart." The deserter laughed in a queer, crazy-sounding way. "Are you smart, gal?"

But he didn't wait for an answer. His eyes narrowed, and his voice turned grim. "It don't bother me none to kill, if I have to." He paused. "But not for generals no more. Understand that? Reb or Yank—it don't matter to me."

Fear flashed through Cassie's body like a fever. Where on earth was Hector?

Struggling against panic, Cassie forced herself to speak. "Listen, I reckon you can't be blamed for deserting." It was a bald-faced lie, but Cassie figured God wouldn't fault her too much for lying under the circumstances. She rushed on. "My pa got drafted to fight with General Lee, and my brother got killed. I sure wish they'd deserted, so they'd be back here with us. See, I understand. You can turn me loose and I won't breathe a word to nobody that I even seen you."

A glint came to the deserter's eyes. "No menfolk around your house, huh? And you got chickens and hogs, I reckon, and a cow. Wouldn't a big old slab of bacon taste fine, after living off roots and rabbits all these weeks? Where you live, girl?"

Land's sake, Cassie thought, *what have I gone and said?* The man was going to rob them of every lick of food they had, and likely cut all their throats to boot.

How could she undo the damage she had done?

"Danged if I ain't lost," she said. "Fact is, I live miles from here. Besides, you wouldn't get no bacon at our house. Yankee foragers hauled off ever' one of our hogs last year. And my brother Philip's a dead shot with a rifle, and my dog Hector, he's mean and he'd tear you up if you come near our place."

"Hah," the deserter said. "Reckon I can handle a scrawny old dog. Ain't a-going to mess with you anyways. Not if you do like I tell you." He stood up. "Take me to your house is all, and fork me out a few necessaries to tide me over till the army clears out of this vicinity." Then he clenched Cassie's arm and prodded her in the back with the knife.

Cassie struggled to break away. "Crazy coot! You think I'd—"

Suddenly the deserter screamed and jerked backward like a dragonfly snatched by a frog. Cassie saw a streak of red fur and a flash of teeth. It was Hector!

Hector sprang and jumped back, sprang again, snarling and snapping, ripping the man's clothes and sinking fangs into flesh. The deserter was yelling. If Hector knew anything, it was how to fight. Wasn't he the best coon dog in the county? The deserter didn't stand a chance. Hector would tree him like a coon or run him off. Cassie knew the best thing she could do was run.

She raced into the woods, but stopped, suddenly, when she heard Hector yelp. Then there was a thud, and dead silence. No sound but the cackling of a crow in the tree above her.

"Hector!" Cassie cried out. Her voice rang through the silence. Frantic thoughts barreled through her mind. *Hector hurt, maybe dead . . . Turn back, try to save him. Yeah, and get yourself killed. Keep on running—there's nothing you can do.*

Cassie wrenched herself away and started running again. Behind her, she heard the deserter crashing through the trees. She picked up her pace, but he was still back there, gaining on her. She could never outrun him; she had to hide. *Where . . . where?*

CHAPTER 4
HOME

Next thing Cassie knew, the ground started sloping downward, and she smelled water—the creek. Like a crack of thunder, it came to her. *She could hide in the caves hollowed out in the creek bank!*

Quakers had dug the caves to hide runaway slaves before the war. The Quakers had all left, gone north when war broke out, but the caves were still there, their mouths hidden under tree roots or in canebrakes. If a person didn't know where the caves were, he would never find them. But Cassie knew where they were, every last one of them. Myron had showed them to her and Jacob and Philip a few years ago when they were fishing with him. Myron was a Methodist, but his wife's people were Quakers, and he'd helped slaves escape before the war.

Cassie sprinted down the slope, purple with violets, and there was the creek—the clear, quiet creek—flowing through the shade of overhanging branches draped with yellow jessamine and bullace vines. Cassie scrambled down the bank and plunged into the water, up to her thighs because of all the recent rain. The icy water stung her belly as she leaned forward and began to swim.

She glided along, quiet as a water moccasin, heading for the black willow tree whose roots were thick as her waist. The roots hugged the bank, and between them was the dug-out cave, smaller than she remembered. She squeezed through the opening, into the darkness. The air smelled damp and musty. She could just barely turn around and face the mouth of the cave. She didn't want to be snuck up on from behind. She lay still and listened to herself breathe. The cave's mouth sliced the daylight into a circle, and shadows played on the walls inside.

After a while, the shadows disappeared, the circle got dark, and she heard thunder, then rain battering the creek bank and plunking into the water. A storm! The creek would rise more, covering her tracks. Maybe the deserter would give up hunting for her altogether.

Cassie hunkered down and got comfortable, as comfortable as a person scrunched up in a cave could be. Didn't the rain, she thought, sound like it did on the roof at home? Her eyelids drooped. After everything she'd been through, she felt exhausted. She thought how the storm would keep Philip from getting his corn planted. And that's the last thing she remembered before she fell asleep.

Cassie jerked awake in a pool of cold water. Inky darkness surrounded her. Her clothes were soaked, and she shivered. Pins and needles darted through her arms. She slithered along her belly through the standing water, toward the mouth of the cave.

A scummy gray sky hung over the blackish forms of the creek bank and trees. Dawn would break soon. It was still raining, but only a drizzle. Below her the creek roared, loud as the beating wings of a flock of geese off a lake.

Cassie dangled her arms from the lip of the cave, and her fingers touched rushing water. She pulled herself farther out of the cave and plunged her whole arm in to test the water's speed. It was fast, very fast. Cassie could swim, but she wasn't sure she was a match for that current. If she dawdled much longer, though, the cave might flood.

Cassie hung on to the willow tree's roots while she eased her legs into the water. The current sucked at her as if she were a licorice drop in the mouth of a giant. Dread thickened inside her. How could she ever make it across? Yet she knew she had to try. If she stayed here, she risked being drowned.

Cassie tore her fingers off the willow roots. Her feet pushed against solid creek bottom. The water covered her chest, almost to her shoulders, and its chill numbed her. She slogged into the torrent. She struggled to keep her balance, taking slow, measured steps. The water pushed and tugged, and several times she lost her footing and nearly panicked. But she locked her eyes on the opposite bank and pushed herself on.

Finally she was close enough to the other side to grab hold of a willow limb that jutted out over the water. She hoisted herself up the steep bank. At the top, she stood for a moment, catching her breath, cold raindrops falling on her face. She thought of the button and felt for it in her pocket. It was gone. She'd lost it in the creek, or maybe in the cave or in the deserter's camp. What difference did it make? The button was the least of her concerns now.

By this time Mama was liable to be worried half to death over Cassie. And what about Hector? Should Cassie go back after him? Her stomach knotted at the thought of going back into that swamp. Besides, she didn't think there was much use. She had an awful feeling that Hector was dead.

And the deserter, where was he? How far had he followed her? Maybe he gave up when her trail disappeared into the creek. Or maybe he walked along through the creek looking for her. Maybe he was looking for her still . . .

The idea made Cassie shudder. Then she grew cold all over as an even worse possibility occurred to her: maybe the deserter had given up on Cassie . . . *and gone looking for her farm.*

A sense of urgency hammered at Cassie. She had to get home and warn Mama. She prayed it wasn't already too late.

Cassie set off at a trot into the woods, her every sense honed to detect any hint of motion that could mean the deserter was nearby. Darkness hung thick in the trees, but the wrens were warbling; daylight wasn't far away. By the time Cassie neared home, the sun was rising over Oak Ridge. It was pink at first, just a tinge on the horizon, and lavender clouds were laid out above like long rows of woolen socks. As the pink deepened, bobwhites began to call out from the woods that edged the field.

Cassie crossed the road, cut through the skirt of pines to the pecan grove, and came up the back way, through the cow pasture, behind the barn and privy. Her nostrils filled with the privy's pungent odor—warm and musky and not unpleasant. A few of Mama's chickens were already scratching for worms in the rich soil behind the privy.

Next to the privy was the barn, and Cassie could look straight through the barn's open doorway and see Philip inside getting ready to milk June, their cow. *Just like normal,* Cassie thought with relief. The deserter had not found the farm. Not yet anyway.

Philip's back was turned. He was tying June to the milking ring on the wall and muttering—muttering about *Cassie*. Cassie hugged the corner of the barn and listened. She couldn't help herself.

"I swear," Philip was saying, "Cassie worries Mama more than all the rest of us put together." He jerked hard at the knot he had just tied, then took the milking pail from its hook and set it beneath June's udder.

Cassie's conscience stabbed at her. Was it true? *Did* she worry Mama that much?

But Philip was going on, stroking June's neck, calming her before he sat down to milk. "Always hell-bent on her own way, that girl is, never giving a thought to the consequences of what she does. She's just like Jacob. Just like him."

Anger instantly replaced Cassie's guilt. How dare Philip talk that way about Jacob! She stormed into the barn. "Durn right I'm like Jacob," she said, "and proud of it."

Philip was startled. He jumped. June was startled, too; her ears twitched and she stamped her feet. Philip swung his head around and studied Cassie up and down, then turned back to June and seated himself on the stool at June's side, as if Cassie weren't even there. He laid a shoulder into June's hindquarter and squeezed a teat with each hand, sending two streams of milk zinging into the pail. "Where you been all night?" he finally said.

Bitterness filled Cassie's throat. "Is that all you got to say? Is that all?" She had had a fool notion that Philip might have been worried about her.

Philip's hands dropped. He turned around on the stool and faced her. His eyes had dark circles under them. "What *should* I say, Cassie? You run off and stay away all night. You get Mama worked up to a frenzy fretting over you. You give nary a thought to the rest of us; you never have. Like Jacob. You're like him in that." A pause. "You two and your devil-may-care attitude. It like to drove Pa to distraction."

Hurt shot through Cassie, but it quickly changed to anger. "You got no business bringing Pa into this," Cassie said. "You're just jealous of me and Jacob. You always was—'cause Jacob picked me to share his secret thicket with instead of you."

"I don't care beans for your stupid old thicket," Philip snapped. "'Tain't nothing but a tangle o' weeds, and it's pure foolishness to make such a fuss over it."

The thicket? Foolishness? Cassie was deeply stung, but she refused to let Philip know. "You sure pined away long and hard," she shot back, "when Jacob wouldn't let you see that tangle o' weeds."

Philip looked injured, and Cassie felt guilty—but only a little. Then, to hurt Philip like he had hurt her, she added, "You're jealous—admit it, Philip—'cause me and Jacob got along so good and the two of *you* never did."

After a long silence, Philip said, "Jealous? Maybe."
For a moment Philip rested his forehead on June's flank,
then lifted his head and went back to milking. "Jacob was
my big brother, too. I worshiped him, same as you did.
Like you still do. Me, I can see his faults now. Don't you
recollect all the taunting we took 'cause Jacob couldn't
make up his mind whether or not to soldier? Jacob was the
only boy in the county who didn't hightail it out to volunteer, and everybody was calling him a coward—"

"Jacob wasn't no coward!" Cassie broke in. "You got
no business saying so."

"I wish you'd quit putting words in my mouth, girl.
I never said he was a coward, only that the really important things, he never could take a stand on one way or
another."

Philip's criticism cut Cassie like shards of glass. "That
ain't true. Jacob *did* take a stand. He joined the army and
fought as good as anybody else—better. You heard that
letter, how brave he was and all."

"Yeah, so brave he got himself killed. A lot of good
it did him." Philip started at the second set of teats,
squeezing, pulling, squeezing, pulling. Cassie felt as if
her heart were being squeezed with each movement of
Philip's hands.

Then Philip made it worse. "Jacob only took a stand
finally," he said, "'cause Emma dared him to."

Angry tears sprang to Cassie's eyes. "You shut your

mouth, Philip. How can you talk like that about Jacob?"

"It's the plain truth, Cassie," Philip said. The streams of milk rang against the side of the pail. "You was too close to Jacob to see how he was."

Cassie was standing with her shoulders squared, her chest heaving up and down. Philip, finished with his milking, rose and set the full pail to the side where June couldn't knock it over. He started untying June from the milking ring.

"I ain't going to talk to you no more," Cassie said.

"Suit yourself," said Philip. He hooked his fingers around June's halter and pulled her toward the barn door, nearly running Cassie over.

"Watch where you're going," she said.

Philip didn't turn around. "You best head on up to the house. You got Mama worried sick."

"I had a good reason why I was gone all night." This Cassie said to Philip's back and the backside of the cow.

"You always do." Philip walked on, leading June out to pasture.

At that moment, Cassie hated Philip. If big-britches Philip knew what Cassie had been through . . .

"Cassie!" It was Emma, up the hill in the door of the chicken house with a basket over her arm. Fetching the eggs, Cassie thought. Emma, her mouth hanging open, was staring at Cassie. "Mama, it's Cassie!" Emma yelled. "Cassie's home!"

The shutters on the kitchen window flew open. Mama's red hands appeared, then her face, beaming. "Don't you move, child!" Mama hollered.

The door slammed, and Mama came running toward Cassie—Mama and Emma both. Cassie ran toward them. She fell into Mama's arms.

"My baby, my baby," Mama kept saying. She was kissing Cassie's head, and her sweet, rough hands were against Cassie's cheeks. It was the old Mama again, the before-the-war Mama.

Cassie wrapped her arms around Mama's neck and pressed her face to the warmth of Mama's skin. She felt tears welling up inside her and spilling over, and she didn't try to stop them. This was the closest thing to happiness Cassie had felt in a long time.

Then Cassie happened to lift her head and look back toward the barn. There was Philip, standing under the overhang of the barn's roof, watching them. His shoulders were thrown back, and his mouth was a tight line.

His eyes met Cassie's. He stared hard at her. But he didn't move toward her. And he wasn't going to, Cassie knew.

The first thing Mama did was whisk Cassie into the kitchen to sit in front of the fire. Next she sent Emma to the house to fetch her rose-and-vine-pattern quilt. "It's the warmest thing we got," Mama said as she set to work fixing Cassie a cup of hot catnip tea. Myron and Ben were at the table, finishing up bowls of grits.

When Emma came back with the quilt, Mama wrapped Cassie in it, stripped off Cassie's wet clothes down to her chemise, and rubbed Cassie's hair dry with the big linen towel Mama saved for company. Last, Mama stuck Cassie's feet in a pan of hot water.

All this time, Mama wouldn't let Cassie speak a word. Every time Cassie opened her mouth to try to talk, Mama clucked and said, "Not a word, child, till that tea is gone. I won't have you coming down with croup or pneumonia or some such thing. Influenza's going around, ain't it, Mr. Myron?"

"Yes, ma'am," Myron said, wiping his mouth on his sleeve. "My Mary"—that was his wife—"been all over the county nursing folks what's down with it."

Cassie tried to bolt down her tea, but it scalded her throat. The best she could do was take hurried sips and listen to Myron. He was telling her how he and Philip had been out half the night hunting for her.

Myron glanced at Philip, who had just come in and was pouring himself a cup of coffee—not real coffee, but the kind everyone made with roasted okra seeds since the war had begun. Philip met Myron's eye briefly, then looked down into his cup.

Myron cleared his throat and went on. "We give up around midnight when the rain got so heavy we couldn't see two feet in front of our faces. I was going to try to scare up a search party this morning, and Philip was going to get some chores done till I come back. But your ma wanted both of us fed and full of hot coffee first. It's a good thing, too, since it don't appear we're going to be needing no search party." Myron smiled in Cassie's direction.

"But, Mr. Sweeney," Cassie said, gulping down her last mouthful of tea, "you do need a search party. Only not for me—for the deserter hiding out in the huckleberry swamp." Then Cassie told her family all about the deserter—how he had threatened her and tried to force her to lead him back to the farm, how Hector had saved her and paid for it with his life, how she had hidden all night in the Quaker cave and nearly drowned trying to cross the flooded creek.

By the time she finished her story, Cassie was almost in tears. Mama sat down on the deacon's bench beside her and clasped Cassie's hand. "Mercy, child, what you been through," she said. "But it's over now. You're home safe."

Cassie couldn't help voicing the anxious feelings that were consuming her. "What if it ain't over, Mama? What if the deserter comes here?"

Cassie saw the worried glance Mama shot Myron, even though she quickly covered it with a smile. "That ain't

likely," said Mama. "How would he find us? And what do
we have that he would want?"

"Food," said Cassie. "All our food. And June. Maybe
even Birdie." Birdie was their mule.

Then Ben, who had been gulping down his third bowl
of grits, suddenly piped up. "Betcha it was him done stole
your ash cake, Mama. I told you it wasn't me. Betcha
it was him."

Ben's statement hit Cassie like a blow. *Could* it have
been the deserter who stole the ash cake? Cassie remembered Ben's tearful protests of his innocence. They had
all just assumed he was guilty; his fondness for ash cakes
was no secret, and there was no one else to blame. A
shiver tingled down Cassie's spine. *But now there was . . .*

A tense silence filled the room. Finally Emma broke
it. She had a horrified look on her face. "Mama, you don't
think it *was* Cassie's deserter who took the ash cake,
do you?"

To Cassie's relief, Mama didn't hesitate a minute.
"No, I don't. Why would a scalawag like that stop at
taking one ash cake off a windowsill?" She paused and
patted Cassie's hand. "We ain't going to fret ourselves
to death over him coming here. It's a good piece to the
huckleberry swamp through thick piney woods. He ain't
likely to find his way to our farm without being led. Still,
just knowing his likes is hanging around makes me ner-
vous. 'Specially with Hector gone. I don't want nobody

in this family traipsing off alone till that man's caught. For no reason. You hear me?"

Cassie and the rest agreed.

Then Mama hugged Cassie. "We come too close to losing something mighty dear to us last night. And we been—I been, anyway—dwelling too much on what's been lost. I'm thanking the good Lord now for preserving to us what he has."

Myron drank the last of his coffee and stood up. "Tell you one thing," he said. "It's plain this deserter feller meant Cassie a lot more harm than he had a chance to do. And I ain't sure we seen the last of him. I'll see what I can do today about getting up a search party to catch the rascal."

Then Myron's voice took on a tone that made Cassie feel cold all over. "Till then, you young'uns stay clear of them piney woods, hear?"

CHAPTER 5
SUSPICIOUS CHARACTERS

As it was, the next day no one in the family had much time for "traipsing off." With April nearly half gone, Mama said, they'd best make haste on getting the garden started. Philip was powerful vexed, too, about not having gotten his corn crop in, so he plowed and planted out in the corn-field from dawn until dusk. Mama didn't like the idea, she said, of him being out there alone, and even though Philip put up a fuss, she made him take the musket and promise to keep it nearby.

Mama wouldn't let Ben out of eyesight, either, while they planted the garden. She put him to work helping Cassie plant onion slips and scallions, which made the whole job take twice as long. The weather had turned even hotter, and the sun pummeled them without mercy. Cassie bent and stooped and hoed until her shoulders felt like fire and every muscle in her body ached.

In truth, though, Cassie was glad to be so busy. It kept her mind off things that were painful and unpleasant—like Jacob being dead and gone, and the chance that the deserter would somehow find their farm. Despite being worn out that night, Cassie didn't sleep well. She woke at every little noise in the loft—the mattress shucks rustling as Emma turned in the bed, and Ben snoring in the bed he shared with Philip on the other side of the curtain. She had nightmares, too, and in the morning she felt as if she hadn't slept at all.

The next evening they finished the garden, and Myron showed up unexpectedly for supper. He brought news, he said—some good, and some that could be either good or bad, depending on how you looked at it. The good news was that his search party had not turned up a single sign of the deserter, though they had combed the swamp and the piney woods for miles around. "Appears the feller got scared when he met up with Cassie, and hightailed it out of the county," Myron said.

The other news was about the war. It was over—or nearly over—due to what had happened April ninth, day before yesterday. General Lee had surrendered to the Yankee general Grant in a little town down east that Cassie had never heard of—a place called Appomattox. Which meant the South had pretty much lost the war. Lee's men, including Pa, would be released on parole to come home.

Myron didn't hold out much hope that General Johnston down in North Carolina could carry on alone for long. Mama and Myron looked serious and talked about the hard times that were likely ahead for the South.

Cassie, though, didn't think times could be much harder than they already were, and at least Pa would be coming home.

Then Myron said he had one more piece of news, special news just for Cassie. He went outside to his wagon, and when he came back in, Cassie's heart leaped. He was carrying Hector—all bandaged up and skinny as a beanpole, but alive! One of the men in the search party had found Hector lying under hydrangea shrubs in the swamp. Cassie ran to Hector and stroked his head while Myron laid him gently on the rug by the hearth. Hector thumped his tail weakly.

Emma was gushing about the war being over and the blockade being lifted. "There'll be real white sugar again—won't there, Mama?—maybe even cloth for new clothes."

"Don't mean there'll be money to pay for 'em," Mama said.

But Emma didn't seem to hear. "The boys'll be coming home," she was saying. Emma had fretted forever that there would be no men left for her to marry by the time the war was over.

Myron held up his hand. "Hold on, girl. It'll take a while for Lee's men to get their parole papers. And won't be no soldiers in this vicinity going home anyhow. General Johnston's got to battle it out with Sherman yet." Both Johnston's Confederate troops and Sherman's Federals were camped a few miles south of Danville, across the Virginia–North Carolina line.

"So," Mama said in her sternest voice, "there'll still be soldiers, Yankee and Confederate, camped all around here. Tempers going to be flaring 'cause of the surrender. And we still got the prisoner-of-war camp right up the road in Danville. There could be more deserters like the one Cassie met up with once the word gets out about Lee's surrender."

"Yes, indeed," said Myron. "Johnston's men'll be dropping their guns in droves and hightailing it home, unofficial-like. Be a heap o' no-gooders looking for trouble."

Myron made them all promise to let him know if they saw any strangers in the woods or suspicious characters about. "Especially soldiers," he said. "Solitary soldiers. Such as them is usually up to mischief."

Cassie shuddered. She knew all too well how right Myron was.

☙

First thing the next morning, Mama set Cassie and Emma to spring-cleaning. Mama wanted everything spotless, she said, to welcome Pa home. All the furniture and mattresses had to be carried out to the yard to air, the shucks in the mattresses fluffed up, the rugs beat out. All the bedding had to be washed, along with every stitch of clothing in the house. There was endless toting and heating up of water, washing and scouring, hanging up of linens and clothes on the line, taking them down and ironing them. At the end of the day, Cassie was bleary-eyed and exhausted.

It was after dark when Mama sent Cassie out to the yard with her big willow basket to gather up the last load of clothes. It was a dark night; a spray of clouds covered the moon and stars. Cassie moved along the garden fence, collecting the britches and dresses and drawers from the line and from the bushes where she had put them when she ran out of room on the line. Her brain was numb with weariness.

Suddenly she stopped, struck by the distinct impression she was being watched. She could almost feel the weight of eyes upon her.

Cassie went rigid. Was there someone hiding behind the currant hedge back of the garden? Or maybe in the toolshed? She stood as still as death, listening. All she heard was a stir of leaves as a breeze rippled through the bushes at the garden's edge.

That's what it was, she decided. Just the wind, and nerves worn to a frazzle by exhaustion.

Cassie realized her arms were aching from holding the heavy basket of clothes. She set the basket down and shook out her arms, still watching the hedge, the quiet, dark hedge. "There's nothing there," she whispered, but her stomach still felt fluttery. Then a whippoorwill called out from the old quince tree beside the well.

"Just a whippoorwill," Cassie said aloud. She picked up the basket and started for the house.

She tried to ignore the feeling of two eyes boring into her back.

CHAPTER 6
MISSING

"Where you been, sugar?" Mama said to Cassie as soon as Cassie walked in the kitchen door. "We been waiting supper on you." Mama set a steaming plate of field peas at Cassie's place at the table. The rest of the family was already seated.

Cassie took a deep breath to calm herself. "Sorry, Mama," she said. "Reckon I'm just moving slow 'cause of tiredness." Here in the warm, lit kitchen, her fright in the garden seemed foolish. She sat down and gulped a swallow of June's warm milk from the tin cup in front of her.

"Cassie," said Emma, "you didn't see Maybelle out there in the yard nowhere, did you?" Maybelle was their wayward hen who liked to lay her speckled eggs everywhere but in the chicken house.

"No," said Cassie with her mouth full. "She run off again?"

"Yeah," said Emma. "She's been missing since this morning."

"I declare, that old biddy has a mind of her own," Mama said. "She's bound and determined—ain't she—to hatch her brood instead of giving us her eggs. If she don't turn up by morning, Emma, you and Cassie going to have to take the musket and go out in the woods to hunt for her. You know she's our best layer, and the way things are, we can't spare no eggs right now."

Emma groaned. "Can't you send Philip with Cassie, Mama? You know I only got two dresses left. If I ruin one out in the woods, I'll have nothing left to . . ." She stopped.

"To cut a figure for the boys coming home from the war," Cassie finished for her. She was going to say more—tease Emma a little about her vanity—but Philip cut in before she had a chance.

"Mama, I can't go," he said. "I still got one, two days left in getting the corn in the ground."

"I know," Mama said. "Emma can go." She turned to Emma. "Why can't you wear that old pair of Jacob's britches you wore to garden in?"

Emma's bottom lip poked out. "Them big, baggy old things *again*? They got that awful red patch in the seat. I feel like an ugly old hag in 'em."

Cassie rolled her eyes. "You ain't going to church in 'em, Emma. Only out in the woods to hunt for Maybelle."

"Oh, all right," Emma huffed.

By morning Maybelle had not returned. Emma complained all through breakfast about having to wear the britches.

So later, when Emma claimed she couldn't find the britches, Cassie thought she was fibbing. Cassie went herself and looked through the chest and all the dresser drawers for the britches. Then it hit her: the britches had been in the load of clothes they washed yesterday afternoon. Cassie distinctly remembered hanging them out on the line. She was sure because she recalled thinking about how Jacob tore them when he climbed to the topmost branches of a persimmon tree to get Cassie some ripe persimmons. The memory had come to her sharp as hoop cheese at Sloan's store, and she'd had to sit down and gather herself to keep from crying.

Cassie told Emma, "I must have missed the britches last night when I was collecting the clothes. I was so wore out, and it was so dark. Likely they're still out by the garden. I'll get 'em." Cassie hurried outside before Emma could question her further. She didn't want to tell Emma about her scare by the hedge last night.

The morning air was cool as clabber but soft with the fragrance of lilacs and cape jasmines. The garden was on the south side of the kitchen, behind the smoke-house. Cassie could see as soon as she rounded the smokehouse that the britches were not on the line or on the bushes. She *had* missed a sock—one of Philip's—that had fallen off a cape jasmine bush onto the ground. She bent to pick it up and then stood for a moment, puzzling over the britches. How could they have just disappeared? Clothes didn't get up on their own and walk away.

Not unless someone walks away with them.

For an awful moment, Cassie wondered if there really *had* been someone hiding behind the hedge last night. Her thoughts jumped back to the previous evening. Maybe she had been too eager to dismiss her feeling . . . because she was too *scared* to check it out.

Well, thought Cassie, taking a deep breath, she would just do it now.

She headed toward the currant hedge, walking along the edge of the garden where the tiny, tender tomato plants sparkled with dew. The freshly turned earth smelled rich and damp. Cassie rounded the hedge slowly, not sure what she would find.

The ground behind the hedge was littered with fallen leaves and twigs from the woods a few feet beyond. But she saw nothing to suggest that anyone had been there last night. Not a footprint, not a broken twig, nothing.

"What a scaredy-cat you're getting to be," Cassie chided herself. "You're worse than Ben." The britches were somewhere in the house, Cassie decided, and would probably show up later, like a lot of things did as soon as you didn't need them anymore.

When another, more thorough search of the house still didn't turn up the britches, Emma, greatly perturbed, had to wear her printed cotton lawn dress into the woods. Cassie had never seen Emma act like such a baby. Emma grumbled and whined with every step. She moved like a snail, holding her skirt up to her knees, pestering Cassie to hold back briers for her, and carrying on and hollering when she walked into a spiderweb. "I swanney," Cassie told Emma. "All the racket you're making, we'll never find Maybelle. You'll scare her off for sure." Cassie would rather have taken Ben.

By the time they reached the spring, Cassie had nearly had it with Emma. The spring was under a huge spreading chinquapin tree and bubbled up from amid a thicket of mulberry bushes. Emma was lagging way behind, and Cassie figured she'd better stop at the spring to wait for her. Cassie scooped up a handful of the cold, clear water and drank it down.

Across the brook formed by the spring was a tangle of blackberry brambles. Its wreaths of white blossoms looked like fallen snow. Cassie had the idea it would be a perfect place for Maybelle to hide. Cassie made her way into the brambles, and sure enough, there was a nest tucked away back in the briers. At first Cassie thought it might have been made by a guinea hen, until she saw that the nest was littered with white feathers. Guinea hens were black and speckled. Maybelle was pure white.

This had to be Maybelle's nest, though there were no eggs in it yet.

"Chicky, chicky, chicky," Cassie called, just like Mama did when she had cracked corn to feed the hens. Maybelle was always the first to come running at mealtime.

But this time Maybelle did not appear. "I told Emma she was going to scare the poor thing off," Cassie said in disgust. "Now I got to be the one to hunt her down." Most likely the hen had only fled her nest temporarily and would come back when she thought the danger had passed. Cassie pushed back farther into the brambles, ignoring the scratches she got from the briers, hoping to find Maybelle.

What Cassie *did* find scared the daylights out of her.

Dangling from a thorn was a fragment of tattered cloth, and from the cloth hung a brass button. It was identical, Cassie was sure, to the button she had found in the secret thicket.

Cassie felt as if her heart had frozen in her chest. With trembling hands, she reached out and pulled the cloth off the thorn. As she did so, the fragment unraveled and fell to shreds. All that remained was the button and a few dark-colored threads clinging to it. She couldn't even tell what color the cloth had been.

Cassie rolled the button in her hand while her mind

raced. *A heap o' no-gooders about,* Myron had said. *And watch out for solitary soldiers. They mean trouble . . .*

Then an image flashed through Cassie's head, an image that made her mouth go dry: the front of the deserter's jacket, tattered and torn, with some of the buttons missing and some hanging practically by threads.

Cassie's pulse pounded so hard she could hear it. Maybe the deserter wasn't gone at all. Maybe he had been here, not long ago, standing in these very brambles. Had this piece of cloth ripped from his uniform when he bent to snatch Maybelle from her nest? Maybe he was here now, this very minute, *watching her.*

Suddenly, behind her, Cassie heard leaves crunching— someone approaching. She whirled around, her heart in her throat, then saw it was only Emma, standing at the edge of the brambles.

"Cassie, darlin', you look like you seen a ghost." Emma's eyebrows were knit together in concern. "What happened? Did you find Maybelle dead?"

Cassie tried to hold her voice steady. "No. I found Maybelle's nest, but she's not in it. Likely she changed her mind and went back home." Cassie glanced nervously around. Was the deserter listening to their every word? She dared not tell Emma about her fears. "Let's get on h—" She started to say *home* but stopped herself. If the deserter *was* listening, the last thing she wanted to do was lead him straight to their farm.

"Let's get on out of here," she corrected herself. She was out of the brambles and pulling Emma back across the brook. In her mind she was already planning a round-about way home to make it hard for the deserter to follow. "Yeah," she told Emma. "Maybelle's probably sitting pretty back in the henhouse. No use fretting over her."

Emma was only too glad to give up the search and go home. The route Cassie chose led through the pine forest, up and down steep hills, but the way was largely clear, un-cluttered by brambles and thickets. There were few places that anyone could have hidden from their view.

Yet Cassie walked silently, and watched. Through thick skirts of cedars and loblollies, past heavy oaks with moss-covered roots, she watched for any sign that someone unfamiliar with these woods had passed. And though she saw nothing, heard nothing unusual, the closer she got to home, the more she was bothered by a feeling . . . the feeling of a *presence* in the woods.

The feeling that something—or someone—was watching *her.*

CHAPTER 7
NOISES

The feeling haunted Cassie into the night. She couldn't stop thinking about it.

Mama had told Cassie not to fret too much over the scrap of cloth. "If your deserter was out there, sugar, don't you know Myron would've found him? That little bit of cloth has likely been hanging in the brambles for months." Mama was worried more, she said, about them not finding Maybelle.

But Cassie kept seeing in her mind that awful glint in the deserter's eyes and hearing him say in his gravelly voice, "Home . . . where might that be?" She kept thinking of the buttons, too, the buttons that were just alike. How could those be only a coincidence? And how could it be only a coincidence that so many things—the ash cake, the hen, the britches—had started to go missing all at the same time?

Cassie knew deep down that it wasn't reasonable to imagine the deserter was behind the disappearances. The deserter wouldn't stop at taking *one* ash cake, anymore than he would stop at taking one hen. That scalawag would take *everything,* just like Mama said. Maybe another no-good soldier was responsible.

Still, Cassie couldn't get the deserter out of her head, and she couldn't sleep. Usually the nighttime noises that carried in through the open window soothed her; now they did nothing but play on her nerves. The *yrp-yrp* of the crickets sounded as loud as pots clattering, and the *boroop-baroop* of the frogs from the pond seemed as loud as a rooster crowing in her bedroom.

Through the usual noises, though, Cassie heard something else: the *click, click* of Hector's toenails on the wooden floor downstairs. That was strange, because Hector never roamed about after the family had gone to bed. He always stayed put in his place by the hearth until Mama let him outside in the morning. Cassie thought it was even stranger now that Hector should be up, since it was only today that he had gotten to the point where he could walk at all.

Something must be worrying him, Cassie thought. Maybe he was hurting, or maybe he was still shook up over the deserter just like she was. Since she couldn't sleep anyway, Cassie decided to go downstairs and sit awhile with Hector.

Cassie slipped out from under the quilts, careful not to jiggle the bed. The mattress rustled, and Emma stirred, but she didn't wake up. Heavy breathing drifted from the other side of the curtain—Philip and Ben, asleep. Cassie crept down the stairs to the front room.

She was immediately glad she had. Poor Hector, for some reason, had gotten up and gone to the door, and then collapsed. Now he was lying on the floor whimpering. Cassie rushed to her dog. "You poor thing," she said tenderly. She lifted Hector to his feet. "You need to go out? Come on. I'll take you."

She opened the door for Hector and followed him out onto the top step. She'd have to help Hector down the stairs, she knew. She went on down and snapped her fingers for him to come.

But Hector didn't make a move to follow. Instead he stood with his nose in the air, sniffing. Then he cocked his one good ear, and a low growl rumbled in his throat.

Cassie felt a stab of alarm. What did Hector hear? She strained her own senses, peering out into the dark yard, listening hard for any sound above the cadence of the crickets and the frogs. Nothing.

Yet there *must* be something out there somewhere, something Cassie in the darkness couldn't see. *At least not from where I'm standing,* Cassie thought, struck suddenly by the idea to climb the tall magnolia tree beside the house. From the top she should be able to see clear to the barn.

Holding her apprehension at bay, Cassie swung her-self up into the magnolia's branches and climbed, easily scaling the limbs that spread like a ladder up the trunk. The magnolia's thick, waxy leaves sprawled all around her, enveloping her.

Then Cassie drew in a sharp breath. Footsteps on the ground below! All her powers of reasoning flew out of her head, replaced by pounding fear. She held her breath, not daring to move . . .

"What in tarnation you doing up in that tree?"

Cassie breathed again. It was only Philip, staring up at her, along with the muzzle of his musket.

"Quit pointing that gun at me," Cassie said.

"You're dang lucky I didn't shoot you, girl. Heard something stirring around out here, come down and found the door wide open, Hector growling—wasn't sure what I'd find up this tree. Git yourself down from there before you fall."

"Will you hush? I was *trying* to see what Hector was flustered about."

"From up a tree? In the dark?"

"I thought . . ." Cassie couldn't finish. Philip made her actions seem foolish.

Then, in an instant, Cassie's embarrassment was forgotten. "Philip! Did you hear that?" she said.

"You mean Hector?"

Hector was growling in earnest now, but that wasn't what Cassie was talking about. "No. It came from the barn."

Philip cocked his head. "Yeah. Sounds like Birdie braying."

Cassie hustled down the tree so fast her thigh got jabbed by a broken limb. "What you think is worrying her? Same thing's worrying Hector?"

"Could be. Wind's rising. Could be they smell a polecat."

"Yeah, could be," Cassie said, almost in a whisper.

"Could be a noise spooked 'em."

"Yeah, but why didn't we hear it?"

"Could be something else spooked 'em." He hesitated. "Like a person."

Cassie suddenly felt queasy.

A cloud moved in front of the moon. Now Cassie could barely see Philip's face, but the white of his night-shirt stood out. His sleeves billowed in the breeze. He started walking.

Cassie was alarmed. "You ain't . . . You ain't going down there?"

"Got to, Cass." Jacob's name for her. It jarred Cassie hearing it from Philip's lips. But she wasn't annoyed—not at all. It felt almost . . . comforting.

"Why?" she said.

At first Philip didn't answer. Then he said, very quietly, "Who else is there to go?"

Yeah, thought Cassie. *Who else is there?*

Not Pa, not Jacob. Just Philip . . . and her.

"I'm going with you," she said. Cassie latched on to Philip's arm and followed him down the hill to the barn. The wind whipped her gown, curling it around her legs. She tried not to shiver. Philip might mistake it for fear.

At the barn they stopped. Its dark, gaping doorway—only an open passageway, really, with stalls on either side—leered at them, as if daring them to go in. Cassie couldn't see a thing inside, but Birdie was still raising a ruckus. June was bellowing, too. *Something* was wrong.

Suddenly Philip stepped forward into the murky darkness of the barn. Panic seized Cassie, and she yanked back on Philip's nightshirt. "Don't go in," she begged in a whisper. "Let's get Myron first."

"Don't be a goose," Philip said, under his breath. "If there *is* somebody in there, by the time we run way over to Myron's, they'll be long gone, with Birdie and June in tow. We gotta go in."

Philip started into the barn. Cassie took a deep breath and followed. Inside, she stopped and waited for her eyes to adjust to the heavier darkness. Philip had stopped just ahead of her. Finally hulks and shapes in the dark shadows of the barn began to come into focus. And *there,* she was sure she saw something, something scrunched up in the corner of an empty stall. It didn't look like anything really, nothing alive, anyway. Maybe it was only a sack of feed, or an overturned washtub.

Philip was walking again, slowly, toward the stall. Cassie took a few hesitant steps behind him, then stopped abruptly. Had the thing in the stall moved? Cassie was afraid to breathe. She thought she'd seen it move, but maybe her eyes were just playing tricks on her.

Except that, then, the thing spoke. "Don't shoot," it said. It unscrunched and stood up. The thing was a tall, skinny boy, about the size of Philip.

"What you doing in our barn?" Cassie demanded.

"Just wanted a warm place to sleep. Ain't up to no mischief." The boy's voice was husky, his accent strange. "I'll be off before daylight." Then he took a step forward. "Ya got anything to eat?"

At that moment, the moon slid out from behind the cloud and gilded the walls of the barn with light. Cassie's and Philip's shadows fell in front of them, and the boy's features jumped into clarity: a thin face, forehead jutting out over large, dark eyes, partially covered by a mass of matted hair.

But what jumped out at Cassie most of all in the

moonlight were the clothes hanging in shreds from the boy's shoulders. Because those clothes were dark blue — the remains of a Federal army uniform.

Philip spoke first. "What d'you know, Cassie? We done found ourselves a Yankee."

Chapter 8

Yankee!

Face-to-face with a Yankee, Cassie thought. *Just like the one who put a bullet into Jacob.* She could feel Philip beside her, shaking, and knew he was thinking the same thing she was.

Her throat felt tight with anger, but she forced herself to speak.

"Appears that way, Philip. Yankee *soldier,* no less."

Philip stuck the musket's muzzle into the Yankee's chest. "How'd you get here, Yank?"

"You got no need for that gun," the Yankee said. "You see me. I got no weapon." He held out his skinny crow-wing arms. "It's the two of you agin' the one of me. And you're armed. I ain't going nowhere. 'Sides, I ain't eaten in days. I'm about as strong as a newborn possum. Wouldn't be no match for you nohow."

"You're lying," Cassie said, for she knew now who had taken the things that had vanished. "You been eating real well. You took my mama's ash cake off the window-sill a few days back and stole our hen just yesterday."

"Yeah," Philip said. "You got some nerve stealing from us, then coming back to bed down in our barn. What was you going to take from us tomorrow?"

"You think I'd come out and steal from Rebs in broad daylight?" the boy said. "I was only passing by a while ago and saw your barn. Thought I'd come in out of the wind and rest a spell. Didn't mean no harm, believe me."

Philip snorted. Cassie didn't swallow the Yankee's story, either, not for a minute. The boy was the thief; she was sure of it. It made her mad that he wouldn't own up to it. "Reckon we wouldn't never believe no Yankee," she spit out.

Philip was still eyeing the boy up and down. "You come on out here, Yank, where we can see you good," he said.

The Yankee obeyed but kept talking. "Listen, I know you don't trust me, but all I'm trying to do is get back home. No more soldiering for me, I swear."

"You ain't only a Yank," Cassie burst out. "You're yellow. A deserter. A skunk."

"No," the boy insisted. "You got me wrong. I didn't run away. Wouldn't do that. Rebs took me prisoner at Winchester. Sent me down here to prison in Danville. I rotted there for I don't know how long, till some of us managed to tunnel out. Now I just want to get along home and see my pa and sisters."

"Where's that? Home?" Philip asked. Cassie noticed he had lowered the musket slightly.

"A farm, like this one, in Ohio," said the boy. "Can I sit? I'm a mite weak."

Philip gestured toward an overturned washtub in the corner. "Yeah. Sit."

The boy eased down on the tub like he was sore just to move. Cassie's anger began to seep away. She had to admit the Yank did look pitiful. His ribs stuck out; his cheeks were hollow. She couldn't blame him too much, she guessed, for taking the ash cake or even Maybelle. "When was the last time you ate?" she asked him. *Besides our hen,* she added silently.

"Don't know 'zactly," the boy said. "Found some slops in a hog trough a couple of days ago."

"You ate what the hogs left?" Cassie couldn't believe anybody could be that hungry.

"Yeah. And was glad to get it. Better than starving."

"I reckon." It didn't seem much better to Cassie.

"What's your name?" asked Philip.

"Name's Gus Baer. Yours?"

"I'm Philip Willis. This is my sister Cassie."

Gus nodded toward Cassie. "Pleased, Cassie." Then he said wistfully, "You wouldn't have nothing to eat, would you?"

Cassie thought with a twinge of resentment of the eggs they wouldn't have with Maybelle gone. But what was the use of going over and over the point with this Yankee? He wasn't going to admit his thieving, and she had to grant that he hadn't done her family any real harm, though he very well could have. It was a relief, after all, to know the thief was just some skinny boy, and not the deserter.

Cassie felt herself softening. The boy had taken only what he needed to live, hadn't he? "We might have something left over from supper we could give you," she said. "But then you got to be off."

Philip was nodding his head, agreeing with Cassie. "There was some cornbread left over, I know," Philip said, "and some field peas. Why don't you go get him some, Cassie? I'll stay here and keep Gus company."

Keep him company? A Yankee? That sounded a little too friendly for Cassie's taste, and it sure didn't sound like Philip. What had happened to Philip's vow to get even with the Yankees for killing Jacob? Cassie couldn't figure Philip, not at all.

For a minute Cassie stood and eyed Philip. Philip met her gaze. "You going to get him something to eat or not?" Philip said.

Cassie's temper flared. "Reckon I will. But don't get too friendly with him, brother. Soon as he eats, we're sending him on his way. Hear me?"

"Yeah," said Philip.

But the way Philip looked at Cassie made her very suspicious. What was he up to?

In the kitchen Cassie put beans in a tin cup and took a slab of cornbread from the pie safe, then dropped them both in a poke sack. She chucked in a few dried apples plucked from the string hung over the windowsill. Last, Cassie stopped at the well and filled a gourd with water. The whole time she was thinking about Philip with that Yankee. Philip was acting peculiar, even for Philip, and it worried Cassie.

When Cassie got back to the barn, she found Philip and the Yank chatting as nice as you please. "You'd think they was kin," Cassie muttered under her breath. It made her mad to think Philip could forget so quickly what the Yankees had done to Jacob.

Cassie strode over to the boy and handed him the food poke. His name might be Gus, but he was still just a Yankee to her. "Here. Eat," she said. Then to Philip she said, "I want to talk to you—alone."

"What about?" asked Philip.

"Don't matter," said Cassie. She shot her brother a look. "I just want to talk to you."

Philip gave her another queer look. Then he shrugged

and said to Gus, "I'll be right back."

Philip followed Cassie to the doorway of the barn, just out of Gus's earshot. "Now, you want to tell me what in Sam Hill is so important?" Philip said.

"I figured *you* had something to tell *me*," Cassie said. "Like why you're all of a sudden so fond of Yankees. It's one just like your Gus who killed our brother. You done forgot that?"

At first Philip didn't say anything. He glanced back at Gus—nervously, Cassie thought, which struck her as odd. When he finally spoke, his voice was unnaturally loud, and he didn't answer Cassie's question at all. "We're going to help Gus get away, Cassie—take him to one of the Quaker caves and hide him for a spell till I get the planting finished. Then we're guiding him through the woods and across the river—get him safe away from Confederate troops and headed north."

Cassie exploded. "Who says we're going to? What you doing, turning traitor? You can't help a Yankee soldier escape. We're still at war, remember? That's treason, Philip—betraying your own country. And it's betraying Pa and Jacob, too."

"No, it ain't. Think about it. What if somebody had helped Jacob? Some Yankee come pick him up off the battleground and nursed him, instead of leaving him there to die? Maybe he'd still be alive. Might be with us now."

Cassie stared at Philip, unable to believe her ears. Who would ever think to hear such a speech from Philip? He'd been more bitter toward the Yankees than she had. She couldn't figure out what had made him change.

But what Philip said made Cassie think. What if some kindhearted Yankee soldier—and it was hard to imagine such a creature—what if some soldier *had* helped Jacob? Would Jacob be alive today?

Cassie looked back at Gus, who was tearing into the food poke like some wild animal. She sighed. "All right, we'll help him escape. But only for Jacob's sake, understand?"

Cassie and Philip took Gus to the creek that night and hid him in the same cave in which Cassie had hid from the deserter. They got him settled, as settled as you could be in a cave, and left him with food enough to last a few days. Though the creek was back to normal now, Cassie cautioned Gus to watch for floods. Philip told him to stay put in the cave, at least during the day. "Last thing you want is to be spotted by Confederate cavalry," Philip warned.

Going back to the caves gave Cassie a strange feeling— part dread, part nerves, and part plain old fear. All she wanted to do was get Gus settled in and leave. That done, Cassie was anxious to get away from the caves—and from that feeling.

"Let's go," she told Philip. Then, without waiting for him, she clambered up the creek bank and plunged into the woods. The clouds had cleared, and the moon was so bright Cassie had no need for the lantern. Yet under the brilliance of the moon, the shadows loomed darker, and the tree trunks shone white. They looked to Cassie like ghosts risen from their graves. The branches crackled in the wind, and an owl hooted from somewhere deep in the woods.

Cassie felt even more disturbed than she had at the caves. She kept thinking about her own words to Philip— *That's treason, betraying your country*—and the more she thought about it, the more sure she became that her first instinct had been the right one. The Yankees were their enemies, had been for the last four years. How could she betray her own people—Pa and Jacob included—to help some Yankee boy, a boy who had already shown himself to be a thief and a liar? For all Cassie knew, this boy could have shot at her very own pa. It might be their Christian duty to feed and clothe their enemy, but it was treason to do anything more.

They should go straight back tomorrow, Cassie decided, and turn Gus loose to find his own way home. She just had to convince Philip that she was right.

Cassie was so lost in thought, she never noticed
Philip passing her. She only noticed all of a sudden that
he was way up ahead.

She yelled to him to wait up, but he wouldn't stop.
He kept right on making tracks toward home, past the
springhouse and the weeping willow beside it whose
spreading leaves always made Cassie think of a lady
dressed for a ball. The willow branches, ghostly silver
in the twilight, stirred slightly in the breeze. Cassie
shivered. She started running and finally caught up with
Philip. She yanked at the tail of his nightshirt sticking
out of his britches, but he jerked away.

"Hold on a minute, will you?" Cassie said. "I got to
tell you something."

"Leave me be," Philip snapped.

"What's sticking in your craw?" Cassie said angrily.
She grabbed hold of Philip's arm and wouldn't let go.
"You cozy up to that Yank and won't even talk to your
own sister."

Then he wheeled around, and the gray-pink dawn
lighted his face. "Cass," he said. "You know what we got
to do."

There was an edge to his voice that held Cassie
prisoner. "What?" she asked.

"It hit me way back in the barn, before we'd said
more'n a few words to him. I've got it all planned out.
It's a way we can fight back against the Yankees, for

what they did to Jacob. It's too bad he turned out to be such a nice fellow, but he *is* a Yankee—"

"Philip, what are you talking about?"

"We got to turn Gus over to our army, Cassie. We got to."

CHAPTER 9
VENGEANCE

Cassie's anger melted away like butter on a hot biscuit, replaced by sheer shock. She was dumbfounded. How in the name of heaven could Philip—dull, work-all-the-time Philip—cook up such a scheme? Plod-along Philip never thought fast on his feet. That was Jacob's style.

Here Cassie was all set to give Philip a talking-to on being a loyal Confederate, when all along he was more devoted than she was. Why, then, did she have this sickening feeling in the pit of her stomach that going along with Philip's plan would only be trading one kind of betrayal for another? Sending the Yankee on his way was one thing. Pretending to be his friend, then handing him over to the Confederate army to be thrown into prison, was another thing entirely.

Then again, thought Cassie, Gus was a Federal soldier. He came down here on his own accord and took up arms against her people. No telling how many southern boys just like Jacob Gus had shot at and killed.

Cassie felt torn apart. How on earth could a person be sure in a war such as this what was wrong and what was right?

While all this was going on in Cassie's mind, she was standing planted under the willow. When a woodpecker swooped out of a hollow right above her head, it startled her. She realized her mouth was hanging open, and Philip was still talking to her.

"There's an infantry encampment about four miles this side of Danville, Myron told me. I figure we can finish the corn by tomorrow evening and set off with Gus after Mama and them are asleep. We'll tell Mama we're leaving before dawn to go to Myron's and help him with his planting."

"Hold on," Cassie said. "I ain't agreed to nothing yet. I got to study on this, all right?"

"Dang it all, Cassie. You pick a fine time to get cautious on me. Since when did you ever take time to study on a thing? Usually you're ready to hurl yourself into the fire and tug all the rest of us in with you. Now, when we get a perfect chance to get back at the Yankees, you don't have the guts to go through with it."

"Ain't a question of guts. I got twice the guts you have."

"Then what's the problem?"

"I'm not sure it's right, is all."

"He's a *Yankee,* Cassie. Look at all they done to us. Look at what they done to Jacob. It's eye for eye and tooth for tooth, like Pastor Hicks preached on last Sunday. Same thing, only this is brother for brother."

Put in that light, Cassie thought, what Philip said made sense. What did one Ohio farm boy matter in a savage war like this one? One less Yank around to kill someone else's brother, that's how she had to look at it.

With the garden planted and the spring-cleaning finished, Mama insisted that everyone pitch in and help Philip with the planting. So the next day, Cassie found herself plowing and planting out in the cornfield under a sun brutally hot for early spring. While she worked, she tried to smother the nagging of her conscience about what she and Philip planned.

Cassie had never felt so bad-tempered. She ached to get the corn in the ground and be finished with what had to be done to Gus. She clammed up and wouldn't talk to anyone, not even Ben, and when he pestered her to take him swimming, and again to help him find birch buds to nibble on, and again to hunt for morel mushrooms, she lost her temper, yelled at him, and made him cry. Then she felt guilty for that on top of everything else.

At sunset, when they finished the corn planting, furious black clouds were rolling across the sky. "It's going to pour tonight," said Mama at supper. She claimed she could smell rain in the air. All Cassie could smell was corn pone and steaming turnips.

Cassie waited for the rain all evening while she worked on knitting a pair of socks for Pa and then while she lay in bed waiting for Emma to drop off to sleep. She kept thinking about Gus in the cave, wondering if he might get trapped by a flood like she had, and feeling bad at the prospect.

Every so often a flash of lightning flooded the room, but it never did rain. When Cassie closed her eyes against the bright flashes of lightning, she saw behind her eyelids rows and rows of plowed red earth. Finally she must have dropped off to sleep because she dreamed about being chased through the woods by something, which at first she thought was wild hogs, but then it was the deserter. She saw his sharp yellow teeth. She thought he had grabbed her and was shaking her. She wondered how he knew her name.

Then suddenly her eyes were open, and it was Philip standing above her shaking her, not the deserter. He looked deadly serious and determined. Cassie didn't know if she was feeling drowsiness or fear, but the last thing in the whole world she wanted to do was get up and go out into that night.

"Come on," Philip whispered. "We got to get a move on. It's long past midnight. Get dressed and come out to the barn. I've got a lantern stashed behind the wagon."

Cassie dressed by moonlight and tiptoed downstairs. She stopped in front of Mama's closed door, she didn't know why. Maybe she was looking for courage, courage to see this thing through. If only she could sort out her feelings, know for sure what was *really* the right thing to do.

Finally, Cassie forced herself away from Mama's door and into the dark sitting room. She looked about the room, gathering in its familiarity: the pine blanket chest against one wall, and the drop-leaf table against the adjacent wall; on the table, Mama's writing box with the mother-of-pearl inlay, and above it, the old planter's clock with pink and blue flowers painted on its face. The walnut armchair was in one corner, and in front of the hearth were the other chairs: the slat-back straight chair with the rush seat, and Mama's rocking chair. On the mantel were the brass candlesticks, the ironstone coffee-pot, and the matching ironstone pitcher that was chipped on the bottom . . .

Wait a minute! Something was missing from the mantel—Jacob's silver mug. Grandpa had sent the mug from Richmond when Jacob, his namesake, was born. It was the most valuable thing in the house, and practically part of Jacob. Now it was gone! Anguish cut Cassie to the quick.

Her anguish, though, immediately turned to anger. It didn't take much imagination to figure out what had happened—Gus had stolen the mug.

Cassie could hardly believe it. She had felt sorry for Gus before because she thought he'd only taken what he needed to survive. Now, to think he had had the mug all along . . . Cassie burned with fury when she thought of him, sitting in the cave, laughing to himself at how easy it had been to fool two ignorant southern bumpkins.

Then she thought of something else, something that planted doubt in her mind. Even though Gus was the logical thief, had he really had an opportunity to steal the mug? He couldn't have had it when they found him; he was wearing rags. It was possible, Cassie supposed, that Gus could have sneaked back to the house while they were all out planting corn, but it wasn't very likely. How could Gus find his way alone through those thick piney woods?

Maybe there was another explanation. But what? *Mama.*

Mama had said only yesterday how hard it was to be reminded of Jacob at every turn. Mama must have taken the mug from the mantel and put it away so it wouldn't make her think of Jacob.

Cassie understood why Mama did it—it felt like a thousand needles pricking Cassie every time Jacob came to her own mind. Still, it hurt Cassie to think that

Mama would remove the mug without saying a word to anyone else.

Suddenly all the grief of losing Jacob welled up fresh in Cassie's heart. Then, just as quickly, her grief turned back to anger. It was the Yankees' fault—all of it was—Yankees just like Gus. It was them that had come down here, invaded Virginia and the rest of the South, and if bad things happened to them here, well, it was nothing more than they had dished out, was it?

Fiercely Cassie pushed aside all her doubts about what they were doing to Gus and hurried out to the barn where Philip was waiting.

CHAPTER 10
GUS'S REVELATION

Cassie and Philip didn't speak as they walked to the caves. The lantern pricked a hole through the black tangle of trees. In its ring of light, Cassie could see Philip shifting his jaw back and forth, back and forth.

"Quit staring at me," he said.

Cassie didn't answer him. She was working too hard to put a name on the feeling that was slowly building inside her. It wasn't fear—not quite—it was more an uneasiness, a gnawing impression that somebody was following them. She kept shooting backward glances, but all she saw outside the lit circle in which they walked was darkness, just darkness. Cassie pressed closer to Philip—he had his hunting knife and the musket—but she said nothing.

When they finally reached the cave, there was no sign of Gus. "Blast," said Philip. "Leave it to a Yankee to disobey orders. Where did that fool get to?"

Cassie was surprised at the way relief washed over her. Gus was gone; now she wouldn't have to—

Then out of the darkness came the Yankee's voice. "Over here. Woke up hungry. Trying to find something to eat."

Cassie looked toward the sound of the voice. The shadows sorted themselves out into skinny Yank against rocky creek bank. He started toward them; his body swayed when he walked, like switch cane on a hillside. "Before the war, a bunch of us boys would sneak out at night in summer and go frog gigging," he said, "build a fire and roast the legs on sticks, then sneak back in before we was even missed."

"Hope you wasn't planning on roasting frog legs tonight," Cassie said. "The smoke from a fire would get you noticed real quick."

"Wouldn't be that much of a fool," Gus said, "though you probably think so, my being a Yank."

Gus picked his way across the rocks and ambled up to Cassie and Philip, grinning. His teeth shone in the dark. An image of the deserter's yellow teeth flashed into Cassie's head. The image disappeared, but the contrast between the two men stuck in Cassie's mind. One Yankee. One Confederate. If you stacked them up side by side and studied on their decency, there would be no contest as to who would come out on top. Cassie's conscience throbbed. She did her best to ignore it.

"No need to hunt frogs," Philip was saying. "We brung you corn pone and a jar of tomato pickles."

"I'm obliged," said Gus. He hooked a pickle with his fingers and gulped it whole. Juice dribbled down his chin. He wiped it with the corn pone he was stuffing into his mouth.

"Mighty good," Gus said. He licked crumbs from the corner of his mouth and stuffed in another pone. Then he spoke with his mouth full. "I was wondering something."

"No more pones right now," Philip said. "We're saving the rest for later."

"No, nothing about the pones," Gus said, munching and swallowing. "I was wondering whether there's any other caves around here."

"Might be," said Cassie. She knew, of course, that there *were* other caves, but she wasn't about to tell the Yankee that. "Why you asking?"

Cassie was taken aback by Gus's reply. "I think," he said, "there may be somebody else hiding nearby."

Philip narrowed his eyes. "What makes you think so?"

"I seen somebody," Gus said. "A man. Only caught a few glimpses of him, but he walked by my cave more'n once, at twilight every time. I made up my mind to follow him one time. I was real careful, waited to poke my head out till he was far enough away that he couldn't see me. Strangest thing, though—one minute I seen him, and the next, he just disappeared. Like he melted into the creek bank."

Cassie's pulse quickened. A man, lurking around the caves?

"What did he look like?" Cassie stammered. "Was he . . . dressed like a soldier?" She couldn't bring herself to put into words the frightening image of the deserter.

"No," Gus said. "Looked like he was from around here."

"What do you mean?" Philip asked. "How could you tell that?"

"Easy," Gus said. "He was dressed just like you— britches and homespun shirt." He nodded toward Philip, and Cassie automatically glanced at her brother, who was, indeed, wearing britches and a homespun shirt. "Only difference," Gus went on, "was *his* britches had a big red patch in the seat."

Cassie sucked in a big breath. *Britches, patched in the seat. Like the ones that had disappeared from their clothesline.*

With her voice shaking, Cassie reminded Philip of the missing britches.

"So?" Philip shrugged. "Lots of folks have patches on their britches."

"Not red patches," Cassie said, frustrated at his indifference. "And not in the seat."

The tension inside her was building. Suddenly every-thing that hadn't made sense before added up in Cassie's mind. The things that had gone missing, the fragment of cloth, the unexplained noises, the funny feelings she had had—they all pointed to one person and one person alone, and it wasn't Gus.

"It's *him*—don't you see?" Cassie went on. "The deserter. Somehow he found our farm, and all this time he's been sneaking around, hiding, waiting to . . . to . . ." She stopped, her throat suddenly as tight as a gorged tick, then finally choked out the words. "I tell you, he's crazy enough to kill us all."

She swiped at the tears running down her cheeks—how could she cry in front of Gus?—and forced herself to calm down. "I don't know for sure I'm right, but it makes me worry, with Mama and them home alone, defenseless."

"I don't know, Cassie," said Philip. "Don't you think you might be jumping to conclusions? How could the deserter have found those caves? Nobody's *ever* found 'em that didn't already know about 'em."

"Philip!" Cassie was exasperated. "Who cares how he done it? Maybe he followed my tracks down to the creek and stumbled onto one of the other caves. I don't rightly know. But I do know I won't rest easy till we scour them other caves and find out for sure if somebody—him or somebody else—been camping in one of 'em."

"I don't think—" Philip started.

Then Gus cut him off. "Listen to her, will you? I don't

know who this deserter is, but if he's as cussed a feller as Cassie says, I don't think you oughta take a chance, not if he's liable to hurt your family."

Gus sticking up for her? For a moment Cassie was startled. But there he was, in all his Yankee-ness, backing her up. "What would it hurt," he was saying, "to check out the caves . . . just to see if anything's there?"

For a long time Philip didn't answer. Cassie figured he was trying to come up with an argument—like usual—but then he sighed, and she knew he was going to give in. "Reckon it might be a good idea after all," he said. "But we'll need more light. We'll wait till just before dawn."

Chapter 11
The Caves

There were a number of caves up and down the creek, all right in the same vicinity, all near the place Gus thought he had seen the man disappear. Cassie and the boys decided to search first the ones that would be easiest for them to locate in the early morning twilight—two dugouts hidden among the switch cane about a quarter of a mile downstream. They also figured these caves would be the most likely ones for a stranger to find. But the first dugout they checked was empty, and the second one had caved in— recently, it appeared.

Philip, staring at the mud slide inside the dugout, turned to Cassie and said, "Reckon you were lucky you weren't in *this* cave the other day, huh?"

"Yeah. Lucky," Cassie answered absently, for another thought had just occurred to her. Gus had mentioned the man "melting into the creek bank." Suddenly she had a good idea which cave the deserter had likely found.

"Philip," Cassie said, "you recollect that cave under the big rock? You know, the rock that sticks out from the bank right over the creek?"

"Yeah?"

Breathlessly, Cassie told him what she was thinking. "That's got to be the one our feller's hiding in. I know it."

Cassie was surprised at how quickly Philip agreed with her. "That rock's only a little farther downstream, ain't it?"

Cassie nodded. "Next to the sweet gum tree with the coon grapes all over it."

"Lead on, girl," Philip said.

Cassie was off at a trot. Soon she spotted the sweet gum, right on the edge of the creek; it was unmistakable. All up and down its huge trunk and into its branches crawled thick, green grapevines. Beneath the tree, protruding from the bank and jutting out over the creek, was a large, jagged stone covered with moss and lichens.

Cassie stopped. Though she wasn't winded, her heart was pounding. Beckoning to the boys, she hunkered down behind a hedge of mock orange shrubs. "There it is," she whispered. "Over across the creek."

The boys crouched behind her. "I don't see no cave," said Gus.

"You can't see it unless you're in the creek, peering straight up at it," Philip said. "And ain't nobody going to do that, unless they know what they're looking for."

Gus let out a low, soft whistle. "I can't believe these caves. You could hide in 'em forever and no one would ever suspect a thing."

A shiver went through Cassie. *No one would ever suspect a thing.* From this cave the deserter could come and go as he pleased. He could do whatever mischief suited him—he could tease and torment Cassie from a distance, sneak into her house, take what he wanted, even Jacob's silver mug—and laugh to himself at his cleverness. He could strike at her and her family whenever he wanted and return to safety here. No wonder Myron's search party had never found the rascal. Who would suspect that a stranger would ever find this cave on his own?

Now Cassie's fear was growing into panic. She fought the urge to run, to put as much distance between her and that crazy deserter as she possibly could. *No!* she told herself. The deserter had done too much already, from invading her secret thicket to invading her home. He had to be stopped before he did anything worse; Cassie didn't want to think about what.

Cassie pushed down her panic and forced resolve into her voice. "Reckon that's what the deserter's been counting on—no one suspecting nothing. And it's up to us to show him different. Likely he's snoozing just as snug as a thieving fox in his den." She hoped she sounded braver than she felt.

"Well, then," said Philip, "what say we go down there and flush the old fox out?"

Cassie chewed on her lip. She did *not* want to go down to that cave, but she would rather die than admit it to Philip or Gus. She drew a deep breath. If she must go, it had better be now—quickly—before she lost her nerve. Without a word, she slipped out from the cover of the bushes and started down the bank.

"Dad blame it!" she heard Philip cussing behind her. "Will you wait for us?"

Cassie paused, just for a second or two. If she waited too long, she knew she could never make herself go on.

Then Philip caught hold of her sleeve, and Cassie thought he was going to pull her back, insist on going first. But all he did was shove the musket into her hands. "You know the way best, Cass, but take the gun. You know how to use it. We'll be right behind you."

Cassie accepted the musket. Even if she had thought of something to say, she probably couldn't have said it— her mouth was like cotton. Cautiously she picked her way down the bank, strewn with rocks and overgrown with weeds, briers, and cattails. Here and there, wildflowers— dogtooth violets, bellwort, wood anemones—nodded above the brush.

Cassie could feel the boys behind her, but she kept her eyes trained on the opposite bank where she knew the cave was. She watched and listened for any sign of movement, any indication that the deserter was hiding inside. The only thing she saw was a kingfisher flitting out of a hole in the bank and skimming across the water. All she heard was the ripple of the creek and the twittering of the birds in the trees.

Now that she was down the bank, Cassie could see the cave, a great black hole yawning underneath the rock. She stopped, every breath coming hard. Her muscles felt tight and uncooperative. She didn't think she could move if she wanted to—which she didn't.

Then Philip nudged her. "What you waiting on?"

Yes, what was she waiting on? For the deserter to poke his head out of the cave and say "Here I am. Come and get me"? What was she so scared of, after all? She wasn't alone and helpless like before. She had the musket. And Philip—she knew she could depend on him, and she realized suddenly that she knew she could depend on Gus, too.

Bracing herself for anything, Cassie crossed the creek, treading from stone to stone. The boys were a few steps behind her. On the other side, beneath the cave, the ground was rocky. A person could come and go, Cassie thought, without leaving tracks or any sign of his passing.

Cassie approached the mouth of the cave, then paused, listening for any sound from within. Behind her, rocks crunched—the boys' footsteps—but from the darkness of the cave, there was only stillness. Cassie squatted and peered inside. She had forgotten how big this cave was. The mouth was narrow, but the cave widened farther back. She could probably stand upright inside, though the boys, she expected, would have to stoop.

The weak early-morning light penetrated only a yard or two beyond the cave's opening, then was swallowed up by gloom. Still, right on the edge of the darkness, Cassie thought she saw something, something white and glistening on the floor of the cave. She squinted, trying to make it out. Maybe it was only stones . . .

She beckoned with her finger to the boys and pointed inside. "What you think that is?" she whispered. "Shining like that?"

Gus shook his head.

"I don't know, neither," Philip whispered back, "but I don't think there's nobody in there. Let's take a look."

"Yeah, let's," said Gus. His voice was eager.

Cassie swallowed hard. Since neither of the boys was moving, she figured they expected her to go first. For a fleeting second, she wished for the old, pushy Philip who wanted her to do nothing but take his orders. Then, trying her best to ignore the queasy feeling in her stomach, Cassie dropped to her hands and knees and crawled through the opening. Philip came behind her, then Gus.

The instant she was inside the cave, Cassie felt her skin prickle from the drop in temperature. She rose to a kneeling position, rubbed her arms to warm them, and waited for her eyes to adjust to the dim light. Then she gasped, for she could tell now what it was that she had seen glistening on the floor.

Eggshells.

CHAPTER 12

TRACKING DOWN
A SCOUNDREL

Goose bumps—not from the cold this time—broke out all over Cassie. *Were these shells from Maybelle's eggs?* There was one way to tell. Cassie scooped up a few shells and brought them close to her face to examine them. It was just too hard to see in this light . . .

"Are the shells speckled?"

Philip's voice startled Cassie. She had been so intent, she hadn't noticed him and Gus beside her. "Can't tell for sure," she said. "It's too dark in here. But I think so."

"Hey!" Gus had ventured a little farther into the cave. "Looks like there's been a fire back here. And somebody done had himself a chicken dinner."

Gus emerged from the darkness holding chicken bones and a handful of white chicken feathers. "Reckon there ain't no more question 'bout what happened to your hen."

Cassie felt something tighten inside her. "Reckon," she said, "there ain't no more question neither 'bout who's been camping in this cave."

"I don't know," said Philip. "I'll allow someone's been camping here, and it appears he stole Maybelle and had her for dinner. I don't see how that proves it was the deserter that done it."

Cassie knew what the proof was—the button from the thicket that matched the one dangling by Maybelle's empty nest. As she explained, the walls of the cave seemed to catch Cassie's words and throw them back at her, dark and grim. When she finished, the boys were silent. Cassie listened to the noises outside the cave: the gurgle of the creek, a squirrel scolding, the tapping of a woodpecker on a tree.

Finally Philip spoke. "How is it you didn't tell us 'bout the buttons to start with?"

Cassie's temper shot up. *Is that all Philip could do? Point fingers and criticize?* She opened her mouth for an angry retort, then clamped it shut. What was the use of fighting like cocks over every little thing?

She sighed. "I don't know, Philip. Reckon I forgot."

"How could you forget such a—"

"What does it matter?" Gus broke in. "She done told us now. And *I* think it all makes sense. Don't you?"

To Cassie's surprise, Philip nodded. "Yeah. Sounds like the old cuss is still around." He paused. "We got to find him before he decides he's tired of playing around and takes a notion to hurt somebody."

"Just how we going to find him?" Gus asked.

"I don't know," Philip said. "Ain't got that part figured out."

"Well, let's do our figuring outside," Cassie said, suddenly cold all over. She wanted to get out of this dark, dank place where the deserter had been, only days or hours ago, feasting on their hen and plotting what he would do next to Cassie and her family.

Philip led the way out of the cave and back across the creek to the cover of the mock orange bushes, where they could talk. Here, with the sun growing stronger and the smell of honeysuckle in the air, Cassie felt warmer . . . but only on the outside. Inside, a cold knot of dread had formed. She knew she would soon have to face the deserter, and the prospect scared her to death.

Cassie and the boys agreed that the best way to catch the deserter was to wait for him to return to one of the places they had known him to be—this cave, the thicket, or the Willis farm.

"It's lucky there's three of us," Philip said. "One to cover each spot."

Cassie glanced uncertainly at Gus. "But he—"

"You still don't trust me?" Gus sounded exasperated.

"No," Cassie said, "'tain't that. I just wasn't sure you'd

want to help us. After the way we treated you. Accusing you of stealing. Not believing you. All that." She stared straight at Philip, hoping he knew what her "all that" really meant. "We should've been more decent to you, Gus. 'Tain't your fault you're a Yankee."

Philip stared hard back at Cassie—he understood what she was saying—then he turned to Gus. "You don't have to help us, Gus, but we'd be obliged if you would. We need you real bad."

"Why, sure I'll help you," said Gus. "You was going to help me, weren't you?"

Cassie glanced at Philip. Gus had trusted them. How could she and Philip have been so false? He was bothered, too; she could see it in his face. "We *will* help you get home," she said, "after all this is over. Ain't that right, Philip?"

Philip answered without a moment's hesitation. "You can count on it."

Gus smiled. "I'm obliged. But first we got to take care of this deserter feller, don't we?" His tone turned serious. "I'll stay here and watch the cave, if you want. But what do I do if he comes back?"

"Reckon you can't do much more than watch him," Philip said. "And follow him if he goes anywhere."

"Keep him in sight," Cassie said. "But don't do nothing more. He'd as soon kill you as look at you."

"Take my knife, just in case," Philip said. He slipped

his hunting knife from its sheath and handed it to Gus. "I'll send Cassie to the thicket with the musket, and I'll go back to the farm to check on Mama, then to Myron's for help. We'll be back to get you before nightfall. I promise."

Cassie's dander flew up. *Who said it was going to be Philip who would check on Mama?* Cassie didn't intend for Philip to *send* her anywhere. If she went to the thicket, she'd go of her own accord. When was Philip going to learn he couldn't boss her anymore?

Cassie glared at Philip. "*One* of us is going back to the farm—it ain't been decided yet who. But we *will* be back to get you, Gus, either way."

Philip was glaring back at Cassie, but she pretended not to notice. "Take care of yourself," she said to Gus. She realized she meant it.

Cassie and Philip left Gus hiding in the sweet gum tree, well concealed by the grapevines.

Then they headed back through the piney woods. Not a trace of yesterday's clouds remained in the sky. The sun was shining brightly now through the delicate green haze of new leaves. A pair of bright orange anglewing butterflies fluttered past on a breeze. It was all in stark contrast to the way Cassie felt: too angry with Philip to talk to him, but wishing she could, wishing she could do *something* to relieve the heaviness of her own anxiety. She couldn't help wondering if the deserter had passed this way just before them, underneath these very trees, on his way to the thicket or to the Willis farm.

Cassie glanced suspiciously around, as if the trees themselves were purposely keeping secrets from her. A big dead hickory tree caught her eye. On one of its limbs sat two huge turkey buzzards. At the very moment Cassie looked at them, the buzzards lifted off the limb, opened their wings, and climbed into the air.

Cassie couldn't help raising her head and watching as the buzzards floated in long curves, without moving a feather—floated down, then up, farther and farther, until they were nothing but tiny specks in the sky. It was a sight she'd seen many times before, but it always filled her with wonder, even now. Up close, turkey buzzards were the ugliest, most ungainly looking birds you could ever see, but when they took to the air . . .

Philip broke into Cassie's musing. "You'd never know from looking at the critters that they was so graceful, would you?"

Cassie was so startled by Philip's almost reading her mind, she forgot she was mad at him. "Reckon you can't tell about too many things just from looking," she said.

"No, you can't," Philip said.

Cassie walked a few steps farther before the force of her own words struck her. And she thought of Gus.

But Philip was talking again. "Reckon the same thing applies to people?"

Cassie jerked her head sharply toward Philip. He was echoing her thoughts . . . again. "You're talking about Gus, ain't you?"

Philip nodded. "We was wrong about him."

"Yeah," Cassie said. "He turned out to be right decent . . . for a Yankee."

"Yeah."

They both fell silent and walked on, through a beech grove and down a steep ravine. Cassie was thinking hard about Gus, how close they had come to doing him a great wrong just because they had judged him by looking at him, like most people judge buzzards. She was so engrossed in her own thoughts, she never heard Philip talking, only noticed suddenly that he had stopped walking and looked angry.

"You going to answer me or not?" he said.

Irritation pinched Cassie. Only a moment ago, the two of them had been talking like . . . almost like Cassie and Jacob used to. And now, here was Philip, ruining it all by lording over her again. "I might answer," she said, "if I knew what it was you asked me."

"I swear, Cassie, don't you ever listen?"

Cassie struggled to contain her anger. She wasn't going to let him draw her into another argument. "Well, I'm listening now." She was trying to keep impatience out of her voice. "What did you say that was so all-fired important?"

Philip looked for a minute like he wasn't going to answer.

He's going to blow up at me, Cassie thought.

Philip glanced away, then back, and finally said, "Why'd you get riled when I told Gus I'd be going back to the farm to check on Mama?"

"'Cause," Cassie said, "you didn't even bother to ask my opinion. You just took for granted it'd be *you* going back to the farm to look out for Mama."

Philip stared hard at Cassie. "I didn't figure there was much choice, since I ain't never been allowed to know exactly where your thicket is."

"Oh." Cassie was taken aback. She'd been so quick to jump on Philip for trying to boss her, the fact that he didn't know where the thicket *was* had completely slipped her mind. "That's right. I forgot."

"You forgot? When all you and Jacob done for years is remind me?" There was no mistaking the pain in Philip's voice.

Suddenly it hit Cassie what Jacob had done to Philip. Philip and Jacob were brothers, only three years apart in age; it should have been *them* who roamed the woods together, *them* who built a secret hideaway in a thicket. That was natural for brothers, wasn't it? But Jacob had taken Cassie under his wing instead. Cassie had always relished the attention and never stopped to think about why it had happened that way. Or how it made Philip feel.

Then Cassie heard Philip's words in her head—
the words that had made her so angry before. *I can see
Jacob's faults now . . .*

All at once Cassie felt a painful tightening in her
chest. She didn't want to think this way about Jacob.
Not now that he was dead and couldn't defend himself.
Not ever.

Then Cassie's eyes rested on Philip, looking so vulner-
able, and a ghost of a memory jumped into her mind. A
memory of herself when she was very young, scared wit-
less by a thunderstorm, bawling, and Philip, still in skirts
himself, hunkered beside her in the trundle bed, wrap-
ping his arms around her, soothing her: "It'll be all right,
baby. It'll be all right." An ache rose up from Cassie's
insides. What had happened to her and Philip in all the
years between?

Then Cassie made a decision. And she knew beyond
a doubt that it was right. "Philip," she said, "the thicket's
right on the way home. Come with me now. Will you?"

CHAPTER 13

A DISCOVERY

Cassie felt tense and breathless as she and Philip started up the hill toward the thicket. Was the deserter hiding inside? When the thicket finally came into view, Cassie's heart gave a little jump. She put out one arm to stop Philip and pointed with the other.

"That's it?" Philip asked.

Cassie nodded.

"How do you get inside?"

"You have to know where the openings are, then pull the vines away and crawl through."

Cassie's stomach lurched. It sounded simple enough — pull the vines away and crawl through. But what would they be crawling through *to*? Was the deserter waiting for them inside that thicket?

With every nerve in her body pulled tight, Cassie took the musket and crept up the hill toward the thicket. She looked for any signs that someone had recently been here—branches snapped off, leaves kicked up, pebbles scattered—but everything appeared just as she had left it nearly a week ago. She tugged at the vines in just the right spot. The vines fell away, and she beckoned to Philip to follow. She cocked the musket, slipped it under her arm, then dropped to all fours and started through. She inched along, an arm first, then a knee, then another arm, another knee, making herself go forward, making herself breathe. Her pulse thudded hard in her throat.

Finally, she had a clear view inside. Her eyes swept across the open space. There was no one there, and nothing seemed disturbed. She relaxed, felt her pulse return to normal. She rose and waited for Philip to come through. Soon his head appeared in the opening.

"Deserter ain't been here," Cassie said. "Don't look like it anyway."

Philip scrambled to his feet. Cassie watched his eyes scan the interior of the thicket—the carpet of leaves, pine needles, and soft green moss, the hollow log, the wall of shrubs and honeysuckle vines that rose above it, all so beautiful to her, so precious—and butterflies stirred in her stomach. She remembered how Jacob had claimed Philip would never appreciate the glory of this spot. "Philip would see it as naught but a patch o' ground and a tangle of vines. And he'd ruin it for both of us." Had Jacob been right?

Philip was screwing his mouth to one side, frowning.

I was wrong to bring him here, Cassie thought. She braced herself for the criticism she knew was coming.

But Philip surprised her. "Tell me again how it happened," he said. "When you found the button. All that."

Philip wasn't even thinking about her precious thicket.

Cassie shook her head. Philip was so unsentimental, so practical. He would probably never see things the same way Cassie did. But now, for some reason, that didn't bother Cassie like it once did.

"There ain't that much to tell," Cassie answered. "Hector come in first, laid himself down by the log. I followed him. Laid myself down. I seen the button when he got up. Somewhere over here." Cassie walked over to the log and propped her foot on it. "Right about here." She shifted her weight to the log to stand on it, but the rotten wood gave way beneath her. Her ankle twisted. She lost her balance and tumbled onto the ground. Pain shot through her ankle and the heels of her hands, but she ignored it and pushed herself up to a sitting position.

She had seen something.

As she was falling, she had seen a flash of color in the hollow of the log, a yellowish-brown color, stark against the dark gray of the log. She had a pretty good idea what it was.

"You all right?" Philip was kneeling beside her.

Her ankle was throbbing. She could feel it swelling.

But she didn't care about that right now. "I'm fine," she lied. "Just got the breath knocked out of me. But, Philip, there's something inside that log."

"Inside the log?"

Cassie, ignoring the stabbing pain in her ankle, pushed herself up to her knees and leaned over the log. Now she could see that she had been right: the color she had seen was a dark butternut, and what she had seen was a uniform, a butternut-colored uniform.

Not only had the deserter been here again, he had stashed his uniform in the hollow of the log.

Cassie felt suddenly light-headed. Here was the confirmation she'd been searching for, the confirmation to all her suspicions. She pulled the uniform out and held it up for Philip to see.

Philip let out a low, soft whistle. "I'll be dad gum."

Now a sense of urgency bore down on Cassie, bore down hard. "This proves it, Philip. The deserter stole Jacob's britches and hid his uniform here, so he could prowl around and watch our farm without folks noticing. He *was* the feller that Gus saw *and* the one camping in the cave *and* the one that took all them things, probably even Jacob's mug."

"Which means he's been in our house," Philip said grimly.

"Yeah," said Cassie, beginning to feel frantic. "And, since he ain't here or back at the cave, it means . . ."

She couldn't go on. Her thoughts frightened her too much.

Philip finished for her. "It means he might just be back at the farm right now."

"We got to hurry then, get back to the farm quick as we can." Cassie tried to rise, but her ankle refused to bear her weight. She squeezed her eyes shut against the pain.

"You ain't going nowhere quick on that ankle," Philip said.

"It don't hurt that much," Cassie said, trying not to grimace. "I'll be just fine once we get moving."

Philip looked doubtful. "I think the best thing is to go right on along the way we planned: I go back to check on Mama and Emma and Ben; you stay here and watch the thicket. One thing this deserter has showed us for sure, he's unpredictable as a mama bear. If he comes back here, somebody needs to be waiting on him. And it makes a heap more sense for it to be you than me."

Cassie couldn't very well argue with him. It was clear she wasn't going far or fast on her ankle. It was already nearly the size of her knee.

"Come on, girl," said Philip. "You take the musket, and we'll get you hid where you can see the thicket real good. Watch yourself, though. Don't take no chances that you don't have to."

Cassie managed a weak smile. Philip knew her too well. "There's a big ol' hollow oak about a stone's throw down the hill. I can hide there." She hesitated. Anxiety was fluttering in her stomach. She dreaded the thought of Philip leaving her here. "You'll come right back to fetch me, won't you?" She hoped her voice didn't betray her nervousness.

"I'll be back before nightfall."

The hollow oak proved a far-from-perfect hiding place. Cassie could only partly see the entrance to the thicket. She also felt as cramped as a walnut in an acorn shell, and since there was no way she could prop her ankle up, it kept right on swelling and hurting like all get-out. She could see a slice of sky, and she marked the passing of time by the way the clouds thickened and fluffed as the afternoon came on. She watched branches bend as birds alighted, and whip upward as they took off. She watched the tender new leaves of the oak lift in the breeze. And so she watched, all that long afternoon— she watched and she worried. About Philip and Mama and the others. About what was happening back at the farm. Even about Gus.

As the afternoon stretched on, and the shadows started to deepen, and the tree frogs started to sing,

Cassie's worry gradually turned to desperation. What had happened to Philip? Why hadn't he come back for her?

Then, out of the corner of her eye, Cassie caught sight of a movement at the entrance to the thicket. She shifted her position to get a better look, and her heart jumped into her throat. There was a figure kneeling to crawl inside the thicket—a figure with a red patch on the seat of his britches!

CHAPTER 14

INVADER IN THE THICKET

Cassie's heart pounded. The deserter had returned, and now that low-down scoundrel was headed inside the thicket. Cassie's mind flooded with all the wrongs the deserter had done to her and her family—the way he had threatened her that day in the swamp and the way he had toyed with her ever since: following her through the woods, sneaking around the farm, pilfering things, coming inside her house.

Cassie's muscles tightened in anger. How could she just sit here and wait, meek as a dove? She *had* to go after him, now, while she had him cornered. She could sneak in through the back passageway and surprise him. "If he tries anything funny," she whispered to herself, "I'll up and shoot him."

Cassie crawled out of the hollow and stood. The pain in her ankle made her dizzy, but, she determined, she *would* get to the thicket, even if she had to do it on all fours. She waited a moment for her head to clear, then took a few hesitant steps. She could walk, though just barely. She crept around to the back of the hill before she approached the thicket, soundlessly, ever so soundlessly. At just the right place, she dropped to her belly and slunk forward, into the back passageway. It was overgrown with woody vines, and she could barely squeeze through. She inched along, musket in front of her, holding her breath, every one of her senses honed. She had to be silent, absolutely silent.

But suddenly—*crunch!* A twig she hadn't seen snapped under her weight. Cassie froze, terrified.

"Who's there?" said a voice from inside the thicket. But it wasn't the voice of the deserter. This voice was rich and smooth, like honey, like, like . . . A wild thought leaped into Cassie's mind. *No, it can't be,* she told herself. *I'm hearing what I want to hear, and it can't be.*

"Who's outside there?" said the voice again.

Cassie's throat constricted; her heart twisted. *It can't be . . . It can't be . . .*

There was movement inside the thicket. Footsteps. Cassie was shaking. Tears were coming. Hands yanked back the branches in front of her.

No one else could have known right where that opening was. No one else.

Jacob! Cassie looked up into her oldest brother's face.

❧

Cassie was seated with her back against a pine tree and her gaze fixed on the brother she'd thought she would never see again. Jacob was much changed from the way Cassie remembered him. Three years ago, when he left for the war, Jacob was a boy of fourteen. Now he was a grown man, with a beard, an ugly scar across his forehead, and weary eyes that belonged in the face of someone much older.

Jacob had settled Cassie on a bed of leaves, with her foot propped up on a stone. He tore off the sleeves of his shirt to make a bandage to support her ankle. Cassie watched as he twisted the cloth into a rectangle and placed it under her heel. He carried the ends up and back, crossed them around her ankle, then went down and around again.

"Where'd you learn to do that?" she asked. She was staring at Jacob, still trying to convince herself that he wasn't a ghost.

"Three years of soldiering learned me a few things," he said. Then he added gravely, "Past killing people."

"We thought *you* was killed," said Cassie. "We got a letter from some major saying you was."

"Y'all thought I was dead?" Jacob's eyes filled with anguish. "Mama must be tore all to pieces."

"Yeah," Cassie said. The lump in her throat wouldn't let her say more.

Jacob shook his head. "I hate you had to go through that. Though I *was* close to dead, I'll allow." He made a hitch under the cloth on each side of Cassie's foot in front of the heel. Then he pulled the ends in opposite directions, crossed them, and tied them. "That oughta do you. You could walk from here to Texas on that." He sat down beside Cassie. "How'd you manage such a savage sprain?"

"Never mind that. How'd *you* manage to come back from the dead?"

Jacob's face looked tormented. "It's a long story, Cass. And you're liable not to think too much of me when you hear it."

"That ain't likely. Couldn't be nothing but proud of you," Cassie said, but a mixture of alarm and uneasiness was creeping through her. What could Jacob possibly tell her that would change the way she thought about him?

"Huh," he said in a bitter tone. "Better hold off *that* judgment till I'm through."

Then Jacob told Cassie his story. His regiment had been with General Johnston, retreating from Sherman's army across North Carolina. The condition of the Confederate troops was miserable—thousands sick and starving, with no proper clothing or supplies. Many soldiers were barefoot, their clothing little more than rags.

"I was one of the lucky ones," Jacob said. "I still had that big ol' gray coat Mama sent me last fall. But this friend of mine—Lonnie Reid—he was bad off sick, coughing something awful, and it was raining like all wrath, and cold, and we was out there right in the midst of it. I was scared he was going to die for sure if he didn't have something to cover him, so I give him my coat.

"Well, next thing you know, we was locked in a skirmish with the Yankees—three of Cox's divisions under General Sherman. They was pounding us with artillery—grape and canister coming at us hard. I got hit, then everything went black."

"But you got your coat back," Cassie said, "before you got hit. You'd have had to, for you to give it to your major when he got wounded."

Jacob looked at her like she was crazy. "What you talking about?"

"That's what the letter said—that you was a hero, pulled that major feller out of danger. Saved his life and then give him your coat. That's what he said you did. Only he was wrong about you being killed. You was just wounded—"

"That wasn't me, Cassie. Must've been Lonnie." Jacob sounded distressed. "Reckon that means Lonnie's dead."

"Then what happened to you?"

"I'm getting to that." Jacob heaved a deep sigh. "Reckon you got to know."

Cassie was starting to be frightened. What had Jacob done?

"When I come to," Jacob continued, "I was laying in a sort of ditch back in a skirt of trees. Weren't no sounds of battle, nothing but birds singing. My head felt like it was near blown clean off, but it couldn't have been, 'cause I was alive and breathing. I crawled out of the ditch, to the edge of the trees, and looked around. The field where we'd been fighting, why, it was swarming with Yankees.

"All I could think about, then, was getting clear of them Yanks. I wasn't about to be taken prisoner. I hightailed it off into the woods, but I must have passed out again. Next thing I knowed, I was waking up in a strange bed inside somebody's farmhouse."

Jacob was burning with fever, he told Cassie, and he drifted in and out of consciousness for days. Finally, the mother of the family nursed him back to health. "She put me in mind so much of Mama," he said, "it made me pine for home something fierce."

When he finally left, Jacob went on, he had every intention of heading back to rejoin his unit. "But I was sick to heaven of fighting. Of slaughtering men like hogs." Jacob closed his eyes, and Cassie wondered what horrors he was seeing behind his lids.

"Oh, Cass," Jacob said when he opened his eyes. The scar on his forehead stood out, red and angry. "How I ached to see you . . . Mama . . . Pa . . . everybody. I could scarcely remember your faces." At that his voice broke.

Cassie's throat was aching.

Then, his face and voice expressionless, Jacob said, "So I changed my mind and headed home instead."

"You deserted?" Cassie couldn't keep the shock out of her voice.

Jacob dropped his head. "It's shameful, I know, but I wanted to see y'all so bad . . ." His voice trailed off.

Cassie didn't know what to say. Her own brother, a deserter.

Jacob must have sensed what Cassie was thinking. He wouldn't look at her. "By the time I got to these woods," he said, "it hit me, the shame of what I done. And the shame it would bring to Mama." Although he was so near to home, he couldn't bear to present himself to the family. Yet he couldn't bring himself to leave.

"So I been hiding in the woods ever since, sometimes sleeping here in the thicket, sometimes in one o' the old Quaker caves down by the creek. You recollect them caves, don't you, Cass? Myron showed 'em to us."

"I recollect." Cassie felt a weight inside her like a stone.

For a moment Jacob was silent. Then he said, "Y'know, I seen you a couple o' times. The first time was when I come and got these britches off the line. You took me by surprise coming out—I had to hide behind the hedge— and, well, I couldn't get up the nerve to show myself."

"That was you." It was a statement, not a question. "You saw me?"

"No, I felt you. Only I didn't know it was you. And I was too scared to go look."

"Sorry I scared you, Cass."

All Cassie could do was nod. She was overwhelmed by what Jacob was telling her.

There was another long pause. Then Jacob went on. "I swore I'd show myself the next time I seen you. But after that you was always with Emma or Philip, and I figured they wouldn't understand, though I hoped *you* might."

Guilt shot through Cassie. She didn't think she did understand. Avoiding Jacob's searching eyes, she asked him about Maybelle. "It was you that took her, wasn't it?"

Jacob nodded. "I'd been living off roots and nuts for I don't know how long, and what fish I could catch without a line. It was Providence, I thought, when I found Maybelle. Figured I could have me some eggs right steady. But I was so hungry, I ended up eating her." He stopped. Cassie figured he was waiting for her to say something, and when she didn't, he went on.

"More'n once," he said, "I wandered to the house all set to show myself, but I couldn't go through with it." Jacob had picked up a pebble and was rolling it around in his hand. "One time I took one of Mama's ash cakes from the windowsill where she'd set 'em out to cool. I couldn't help it—I remembered how good they was, and I was just so hungry, Cass."

Though he was staring at the pebble and not looking at Cassie, she heard the pleading in his voice. She knew he was desperate for her to understand.

"Mama give Ben a whipping for taking that ash cake," Cassie heard herself say. It came out sounding hard and harsh, not at all like Cassie had meant it. Jacob's face fell.

"Little ol' Ben got a whipping on my account." He shook his head. "I should have gone on and left—gone off to start a new life somewhere. I seen that, finally, since it was clear I wasn't never going to get up the courage to show myself to Mama, and I wasn't about to go back to the army and risk being shot for deserting."

Cassie shuddered. It wasn't so long ago that she had declared a bullet was what a deserter deserved.

"Yesterday," Jacob said, "when I seen y'all out in the cornfield, I snuck in the house and took my silver mug from the mantel." He lifted his head, and his tone turned defiant, more like the Jacob Cassie remembered. "I figured it was mine anyway, and it'd bring a heap o' money in Danville or Greensboro. Enough so I could head out west—Texas, maybe even California.

"Even so, it was almighty hard to make myself leave, without saying good-bye, knowing I couldn't never come back. I told myself I'd spend one last night in the thicket and then I *had* to be off—for good. Only I didn't expect to run smack into you."

Cassie was in turmoil. There were so many feelings tumbling around inside her, and she couldn't put a name on any of them. She had never felt so confused in her whole life.

But Jacob was looking right at her, with those clear blue eyes of his. She had to say something. "Ain't no need to go away if you don't want to. General Lee done surrendered. War's all but over."

A brief spark came to Jacob's eyes. "Ol' Marse Robert surrendered, huh? Then Johnston can't last much longer."

"Folks won't know you deserted," Cassie went on. "They'll just think you been paroled and made it home quicker'n everybody else."

Jacob's face clouded. "What? And have to lie about what I done for the rest of my life? I'd rather leave, I think." He paused. "Cass? You think Mama would be ashamed of me if I did go home? And Pa?"

Cassie didn't answer. What would it be like, she thought, if everyone knew her brother was a deserter? She dropped her eyes.

Pain filled Jacob's face. "*You're* ashamed of me, ain't you, Cassie?"

Suddenly Cassie's breathing came hard. *Was* she ashamed of Jacob? She had worshiped him ever since she could remember . . . Her chest ached at the thought.

Then she remembered the buzzards. And Gus.

Names attached to things—or people—didn't change

what they were deep down. Yankee. Deserter. They were only names. Names that didn't really tell you much of anything, when you got right down to it.

Maybe Philip was right. Maybe it *was* Cassie who had never been able to see Jacob clearly. So Jacob *wasn't* perfect, like she had thought. So he had faults. That made him like everybody else, didn't it?

Deserter or not, Jacob was still the same person he had always been. Her brother.

"No," Cassie said. She was looking straight at Jacob now. "I ain't ashamed of you."

CHAPTER 15
HOMECOMING

Jacob stayed two weeks after he came home, long enough to take Gus into Danville and put him on a train to Ohio, and long enough to help Philip plant three more acres of corn and an acre of sweet potatoes. It rained on the day Jacob left for California. Mama said it was fitting that the sky should cry on the day that she lost her oldest boy for the second time.

In one way, Cassie understood why Jacob had to go; in another way, she didn't. None of them, Mama least of all, held against Jacob what he had done, but Cassie thought he held it against himself. The note he left for Mama pretty much said so.

Jacob slipped away before dawn one morning, while everybody was sleeping. All he left behind was the note for Mama and a little wood carving of Hector for Cassie. Later, when Philip got up, he told Mama that Jacob had never intended to stay. "He told me so," Philip said, "'long about the third or fourth day when we was planting."

"He told *you*?" Cassie was stung to the quick. Why would Jacob tell Philip about his plans and not tell her?

"Yeah, he told me. We talked a lot out there in the field while we was working side by side. Jacob said it was plain to see I was smart as a steel trap when it come to farming." Philip's eyes were shining. Envy stabbed at Cassie.

Philip went on. "Jacob said he wasn't never smart that way, and Pa seen it and favored me. It ate away at him, he said, and he figured he took it out on me without meaning to."

"Pure foolishness," Mama broke in. "Your pa never favored one young'un over the other."

"I ain't saying it's true, Mama," Philip said quietly. "I'm only telling you what Jacob told me. He said he always had the feeling he didn't measure up to what Pa wanted, and that's why he joined the army—to try to make Pa proud of him. And that's why he said he couldn't stay. 'Cause he couldn't bear to see Pa's face when Pa found out he deserted."

"Why didn't you tell this to nobody before?" said Cassie. "We could have told Jacob he was wrong and stopped him from going!"

"That's just it, Cassie. He didn't want to be stopped. There's some things a man has got to do; he knew I seen that and you wouldn't." Philip's eyes held sympathy. "It wasn't because he felt any different toward you than he ever did."

At first Cassie was hurt, but the more she thought about it, the more she understood. It seemed better in a way that Jacob should confide in Philip. It set things right between her two brothers at last, set things to the way they should have been all along.

Two days later Mama came home from Sloan's store with news of General Johnston's surrender. She said the war was over for good now, and folks at the store were saying that the trains arriving in Danville were already packed with soldiers coming home.

Soldiers coming home . . . coming home . . . The words echoed in Cassie's head. If Jacob hadn't deserted, *he'd* be one of them. Cassie closed her eyes and pictured it in her mind: a dark night, a knock on the door, and Jacob standing there on the step—how wonderful—when they all had thought he was dead! And later, when Pa made it home from Appomattox, the whole family would be together again, just like before the war.

Cassie couldn't bear thinking like that. Finally, there was nothing she could do but take Hector and head for the woods. It was late in the afternoon, after chores but before supper. They took the wagon path through the orchard. The sun hung low in the creamy blooms of the apple trees.

Hector trotted at Cassie's heels. He seemed completely healed from his fight with the deserter. His ears—one of them crooked now—were perked up, and his nose was in the air, waiting to catch wind of a rabbit. Cassie felt downcast and restless, and she dawdled along the path, picking blossoms from the trees, throwing sticks for Hector, trying to ignore her gloomy thoughts.

All of a sudden a gray squirrel scurried across the path, and Hector bounded after it. The squirrel ran up the trunk of the tallest apple tree and sat just out of Hector's reach, chattering and scolding. Hector set into a frenzy of barking and jumping.

Even through her mood, Cassie couldn't help being amused. "That old squirrel is acting right sassy, ain't he, boy?" she said to Hector. Hector yipped and looked at her imploringly. His wagging tail whipped against the tree trunk.

"Ahh," Cassie said, "you want me to teach him some manners. Reckon I could do that for a good friend like you." She caught onto a low limb of the tree and swung into its snowy branches. The squirrel scampered up out of her reach.

Then a breeze kicked up, the branches trembled, and a rain of blossoms floated down and landed in Cassie's hair and on her dress. The sweet smell of flowering apples filled Cassie's nostrils. Above her and below her and all around her was a sea of white, so pure and clean, Cassie's mood suddenly lifted.

She started to climb; she climbed higher than she should have. It felt good to be up so high, above the world and its troubles. She scooted closer to the trunk, held tight to it, and looked out across the landscape.

In the west, far across the woods, was the river, and the huge orange ball of the sun, suspended, ready to drop into the water. In the opposite direction, the last of the sunlight was scattered across Oak Ridge. Dusk was coming on fast. The piney woods and the pecan grove were already dark, and the stretch of road in between was fading quickly away. But Cassie could see a shadow moving through the pines where she knew the road was—a shadow that looked like a horse and wagon.

Who would be coming way out here with a wagon this late in the evening? It had to be Myron, but why?

"Reckon I'll just find out," Cassie said aloud. She clambered down the tree and took off running, Hector behind her. She reached the fork in the road before the wagon did, so she perched on the old rock wall to wait. The tree frogs had started to sing, and thick darkness was gathering all around her.

Soon the wagon appeared out of the pines. In the dark, Cassie wouldn't have known Myron was driving the wagon, except that she recognized Lucy's slow, plodding gait. All Cassie could see were shapes—one shape that was Myron's, holding the reins, and the shape of someone else beside him. Cassie couldn't tell who the other shape was. The *glup-glup* of Lucy's hooves in the mud got louder; the wagon drew closer.

What happened then would always be a blur to Cassie. She heard the wagon wheels rattling. She heard Hector barking. She heard voices—Myron's and another voice, one that was familiar, so familiar. All of a sudden Cassie was running toward the wagon. She jumped on, and she felt her father's arms around her. Myron was laughing, saying something. Cassie didn't hear him. All she heard was Pa saying her name. And she was crying.

The next thing that was clear in Cassie's mind was the wagon pulling through the pecan grove with the lit windows of their farmhouse cutting through the dark up ahead. Pa moaned. "Oh, what a sight," he said. "What a purty sight." He squeezed his arm tight around Cassie's shoulder. "Time was when I allowed I'd never see home again. Now I'm here with my Cassie girl, so near to home I can taste it."

He turned to Myron. "Sweeney, you know what I want first thing after I hug my wife and babies?"

"What's that, Willis?"

"You recollect what I told you was the one victual I hankered for down those long roads on my way home?"

Myron laughed and bellowed out, "Poke salad!"

Pa kissed the top of Cassie's head. "Reckon your mama would fix me up a mess of poke salad?"

Cassie brushed her face against Pa's woolly beard. She thought about Mama's vow that she'd never make poke salad again, and all that had happened since. They had lost Jacob and gotten him back, only to lose him again. And in the short time Jacob had been home, he'd never asked for poke salad, not once. *Would* Mama make poke salad for Pa? Cassie didn't know. But she didn't want to say anything that would spoil Pa's happiness—or her own. "Reckon Mama would do anything for you," she told Pa.

Then they were home—Cassie had never even had time to picture what it would be like. The wagon pulled up in front of the house. Pa jumped down and slung Cassie down with him. They ran to the door, and they were inside. Everybody was there. Pa picked Mama up and swung her around. Tears streamed down Mama's face, but she didn't seem the least bit embarrassed. Pa slapped Philip on the back, like Cassie had seen him do the men-folk at the store. Pa hugged Emma, told her she was the spitting image of Mama at sixteen, which made Emma start spouting tears like a watering can. And little Ben got a ride on Pa's shoulders.

That night at supper, Mama told Cassie she had an errand for her first thing in the morning.

"What you want me to do, Mama?" Cassie asked.

"I want you to take a basket and hunt me the tenderest, greenest poke shoots you can find. I aim to make your pa some poke salad for supper tomorrow."

Cassie couldn't believe her ears. She looked at Pa. Pa winked at her, and Mama smiled, a big smile that made her face look like the sunrise over Oak Ridge.

1865

GOING BACK
IN TIME

Looking Back: 1865

By the spring of 1865, when Cassie's story takes place, it had been four long years since the country split in two in the bloody conflict we know as the Civil War. The storm that erupted on April 12, 1861, over Fort Sumter, South Carolina, had been brewing for a long time.

For years the North and the South had behaved like quarrelsome siblings, bickering over which region should have the most power in government—which should be the "boss." Since the North had more money, people, factories, and businesses, it sometimes acted like the "big sister," trying to force the South to "do things my way." The South, in turn, would threaten to *secede*—to declare its independence and form a separate nation—if the North didn't give in to it. One of the biggest arguments had to do with slavery. Many people in the North wanted to end slavery, but the wealthiest and most powerful Southerners relied on slave labor to run their vast plantations.

In 1861, the South made good on its threats and seceded, declaring itself the Confederate States of America. The North, led by President Abraham Lincoln, was determined to keep the United States from breaking up. Lincoln sent Federal troops to try to force the Confederacy back into the Union.

The Confederate army was not filled with wealthy slave owners, however. Soldiers were mostly laborers and *yeoman farmers* like Pa and Jacob—men who owned only a few acres of land and had no slaves. These men went to war not to preserve slavery but to protect their homes and families from the Northern invaders.

At first, neither side believed the other was truly serious about the war. Most people thought the fighting would be over quickly. Full of excitement and patriotism, young men on both sides rushed to join *militias,* or local military groups. With parades and celebrations, communities outfitted their militias and grandly sent them off to "whip the enemy." Sisters and girlfriends urged hesitant brothers and sweethearts to volunteer, just as Emma did with Jacob.

Like Jacob, many who volunteered were mere boys. Confederate Charles Carter Hay enlisted in 1861 at age 11; when he surrendered in 1865, he was one month shy of his 15th birthday. A young private from Texas was 13 when he lost a leg in battle. Drummer boys and musicians were sometimes as young as 9 or 10.

But the war did not end quickly. Months dragged on into years, and the war turned bloody. Fewer and fewer men volunteered to fight. Both sides began to draft soldiers. Husbands and fathers, like Cassie's pa, were forced to go to war, leaving their families to fend for themselves.

Because almost all the fighting took place in the South, the war took an especially terrible toll on women and children there. Fields and backyards became battlefields. Houses and farms were destroyed. To supply their troops, Federal armies foraged the countryside, taking food and supplies from local families without paying for it. Soldiers sometimes looted homes for valuables, then burned anything they didn't take. Destroying towns, cities, and farmland became a policy of some Northern generals late in the war. Philip Sheridan's troops devastated Virginia's Shenandoah Valley, and William Tecumseh Sherman set out to "make Georgia howl." As marching armies drew near, frightened families fled. Many were left homeless and destitute.

Even in areas farther from the fighting, times were hard. Women like Cassie's mother and boys like Philip struggled to keep farms running. "No-good soldiers" like the ones Mama warned Cassie about roamed the countryside, stealing and committing acts of violence against civilians. Money was in short supply, and with Southern ports blockaded by Northern ships, all goods were scarce. Basic items like sugar, coffee, nails, writing paper, and fabric either disappeared from stores or cost so much that no one could afford them. Townspeople, unable to produce their own food, suffered the most. Toward the end of the war, food prices were sky-high. Flour sold for as much as $1,000 a barrel. Many families were near starvation. In some southern cities, citizens were reduced to eating rats.

Things were not much better for Confederate soldiers. Johnny Reb, as Southern soldiers were called, might live for days on nothing but crackers called *hardtack*. Sometimes there was not even that. One soldier wrote to his father, "What is to become of this army without rations. Men can't fight on nothing to eat." Men did fight, though—hungry, often barefoot, and with their clothing in rags. It was the lucky Reb who had a coat or blanket to keep off the wind and rain and to see him through the winter. It is no wonder that more soldiers died from sickness than were killed in battle.

Though comforts were greater for the Union soldier—Billy Yank—he also faced the daily threat of dying in battle. Some soldiers decided they could no longer take it all and *deserted,* or ran away from the army. Deserters who were caught faced the death penalty. Even if a deserter wasn't caught, he risked being scorned by his family and community. People in those days greatly valued duty, honor, and reputation. They considered a coward or deserter a disgrace to the family.

Late in the war, however, many people changed their attitudes as they grew desperate for their men to come home. Some wives even wrote letters to their husbands, and mothers to their sons, begging them to desert. One heartrending letter tells a father how his children cry from hunger and grow thinner by the day. "Please, Edward," his wife begs, "unless you come home we must die."

Eventually, so many Confederate soldiers deserted that it helped bring about that army's collapse. The end came in April 1865, when Robert E. Lee surrendered to Ulysses S. Grant at Appomattox, Virginia, and a few weeks later Joseph Johnston surrendered to Sherman in North Carolina.

With the South's defeat, the North achieved its goal of preserving the nation. Slavery also came to an end. But the cost was agonizing. The Civil War claimed more than 500,000 lives and left the South in ruins.

About the Author

While she was growing up, Elizabeth McDavid Jones spent many hours in the piney woods near her home in North Carolina. Whether playing with her friends or lolling on the creek bank writing poetry, she was happiest when she was outdoors.

That hasn't changed now that she's an adult. Whenever she can, she loves getting away with her husband, five children, and their dog to hike, canoe, or camp. They live in the foothills of central Virginia.

"Liz" is also the author of six other historical mysteries for children: *The Night Flyers, Secrets on 26th Street, Ghost Light on Graveyard Shoal, Mystery on Skull Island, Peril at King's Creek,* and *Traitor in Williamsburg.* In 2000, *The Night Flyers* won the Edgar Allan Poe Award for Best Juvenile Mystery. *Ghost Light on Graveyard Shoal* was an Agatha Award Finalist.